TINNITUS

Sound is the weapon
Noise is the crime

TINNITUS

Jack Calverley

The Logic of Dreams

For a brief time I was here;
and for a brief time I mattered.

Harlan Ellison

Acknowledgements

I would like to express my thanks to Sue Jenkins for reading the first full draft of this manuscript and catching errors of all sorts, and I would like to say my special thanks to my good friends Sanja Baletic and Julian Dixon for all their support during the writing and production of this novel.

Jack Calverley

PROLOGUE

Jennifer opened the office window. There'd been a smattering of rain overnight and everything about the farm was ripe. She adored the smell of freshly cut hay. "Did you see the letter from Ruby Murray?"

"Ruby Rattler," Callum corrected her.

The clank of metal from the gloom of the adjoining workshop told her he was going through the heavy machinery toolbox.

"Whatever," she said. "Looked urgent." The words 'First Class' had been double underlined on the front of today's mauve envelope.

"*Whoever*, but yes."

"And?"

"Swimming pool job," he said. "We got any of those dodgy pumps left?"

"Probably," she said.

"Thanks. There were some old headphones, somewhere, as well..."

"Will you be long?" The red nose of a Porsche Convertible poked out from the small barn. She fancied taking it for a spin. Except he had first dibs. "Only, just so you know, I'll be finishing early today," she said, "headed for town—to see *Gaius*."

"*Again?* Didn't know that thing was still going."

1

"It isn't. It's a one-off. A charity event. All the hits, live, it says, and much of the original orchestra—even some of the original cast..." She realised the *faux pas* too late, cringed and clamped her mouth shut.

"You seen Brain Damage?"

Maybe he hadn't heard. She could hope. She said, "I wish you wouldn't call it that. The jumbo spanner is wedged in the cat flap to keep it open. Which you could fix, by the way, now you're calling yourself semi-retired."

"There is no retiring," he said, wearily. "Leastways, not today. I'm taking Brain Damage with me."

"Where?"

"Morricone Crescent. Notting Hill no less. I'll crash at Charlie's."

She said, "You were going to take up painting."

"Yeah, well, after this one, who knows."

"You've said that before. I've yet to see an easel." She turned as he came into the office and watched as he meticulously placed the tools of his trade into a spotlessly clean sports bag. "Be safe," she said.

"This one's for Evie," he said. "The Good Lord is on my side."

"Oh—" Jennifer felt a twinge of shame. Callum's sister had been an actress in the original cast of *Gaius*, but she'd killed herself when some bastard conned her out of her life savings—and she a Catholic. Then, suddenly, feeling incredibly dense, Jennifer realised precisely what Callum had said: "You mean, you've found him?"

"Not me, Ruby Rattler. I got Ruby Rattler to thank."

"Oh!"

"Oh, indeed," he said. "Poetic justice, I'm thinking. You taking a trip down memory lane with Gaius. Me taking a trip down memory lane with Gaius. You get to see a brutal stabbing. But I get to see, well— we'll see, won't we—what I get to see. Never cross a Doherty that's for sure. Never a Doherty. Always a bad idea, that."

CHAPTER ONE

Sandy Amadeus arrived at a quarter to nine even though the woman had said, "About nine," and not to worry. "It's difficult to find."

In the narrow lobby he now risked straining his voice to make himself heard above the ghetto-blaster on the floor which was playing house music and above the relentless banging of a hammer on the far side of a nearby wall:

"Vic Victor!" He felt like his throat would scratch itself dry. "I'm looking for Vic Victor!"

The guy behind reception had scarlet headphones clamped to his ears and continued to stand, motionless, staring at the screen of a desktop computer that was perched on the counter. He wore his hair straggly and black (showing at the roots) and was definitely on the anorexic side of wiry but trying to appear bigger than he was under a loose, age-creased black leather jacket.

Sandy couldn't have been more obviously in front of the guy and had to wonder whether being ignored was the penalty for getting close enough to be noticed.

A scatter of freebie magazines littered the counter a little farther along. Most of them had Princess Diana on the cover, although one showed an advertisement for *Phantom* on the back.

However, Sandy wasn't looking to kill time until someone came for him.

The counter hugged one side of a flaking, white-painted corridor that was badly lit and led off into the building. He felt stirred to the brink of action, but you couldn't just walk in, could you?

Behind him, every so often, a body would jostle past, hefting a tea chest out of the building. Shortly after, a different body, wiping hands on jeans and pointedly squeezing through sideways, would pass by in the opposite direction.

Sandy decided he couldn't stay here.

Minutes ago, from the outside, the glass-fronted building which was no wider than a sandwich shop had mirrored the trees of Hoxton Square, with their black and grey trunks and greenery that, presumably for the whole summer, would conceal the broken-windowed warehouse opposite. In the bright sunlight of that Monday morning, the outside of the building displayed all the promise of something ultra modern and elegantly cool.

Inside however, the building ran only to gloom, the mousey scent of tea chest wood and an unending, nail-screeching din.

A floppy-haired young woman was the next person to enter the building and when she turned sideways to pass him, Sandy put his arm out to stop her. She had apple-pink cheeks, watery blue eyes, wore a *Cats* tee-shirt, and was hardly any older than he was.

Leaning into her ear, he raised his voice, "Vic Victor?"

Against the din, in a Liverpool accent, she said, "Next door kiddo!" But she jabbed her finger in the direction she was headed, deeper into the building. "Make yourself useful!"

Sandy had spent over an hour that morning finding a look to suit the occasion. He had ironed his mustard yellow shirt, untangled his bootlace tie—even polished its silver guitar clasp—and had carefully brushed dog hairs and fragments of rosin from his grey paisley waistcoat. He wanted to capture something of the authentic Western *bolo and vest*, yet add his own touch of jazz. The showman, the performer, that was the first impression he needed to make. Finally he had tied his ponytail with a dark brown bungee that exactly matched the colour of his hair, but he decided that any kind of a hat would undermine the casualness of his urban cool.

In his head, and in the mirror, he had rehearsed and revised the posture and the voice of the creature he wanted to be: the professional musician who took life in his stride while always on the lookout for an exciting—no, an ambitious—no, no, sir, mister Victor, sir, that is to say sir, an *unmissable*—new musical.

Never mind that Sandy had to scrape pennies together to help his mother meet her rent—and pay his own—while struggling to stay in the industry, to keep that foot in the door. Any work, any time, any place: he would do it. *Just set me down close to the stage, close enough to smell the sweat. I will do the rest.*

But now, with this young woman's request to be

useful he saw only dust, dirt, breathless dishevelment and—when called upon to sing—fits of coughing. The failure of his audition loomed large. The failure of this chance of a lifetime. The only First Impression he would ever make on the indomitable Vic Victor and the one time he needed *not* to get his hands dirty. Yet he had to show willing if his ambition was to join this famously hands-on company.

With a theatrical gesture, he accepted her invitation.

At the back of the building, beyond a concealed stairwell, he came to a single large room and faced a wall-sized, metal-framed window that allowed the morning sunlight to flood in.

A middle-aged woman in a blue boiler suit, with a wide, dimpled face and her hair up, was lifting box files in threes and fours from the lowest shelf of a metal rack and dropping them into the last in a row of tea chests. She paused, and said, "Someone take the weapons, will you? Can't find any more."

Sandy peeked into the tea chest closest the door, which he had thought empty, and discovered a collection of hand guns and stage daggers at the bottom. He contrived to lift the chest while minimising any contact with his clothes. It was deceptively heavy. He just hoped he didn't have to carry it far.

'Next door' turned out to be a double-width building three doors along, up one flight of steps outside, and up three flights of stairs inside. In the brief pauses for door-openings and door-kickings-shut he established that the young woman with the watery blue eyes and *Cats* tee-shirt called herself Pauline, and the company was being forced out of their office.

When eventually he reached it, he found the whole of the top floor 'next door' was given over to a single, gable-ceilinged room. An open French window let air in at the front while a row of metal-framed windows let the sun in at the back. Thankfully, he had left all the noise of the street at street level. The hammering was barely audible. The ghetto-blaster not at all. You could hardly hear any traffic, either from the Square or from the streets nearby. The only real sound came from two people sharing a desk under the window at the back, quietly talking on their phones.

The air was filled with the smell of freshly ground coffee, but for now that was a luxury he would have to forego. He added his tea chest to an orderly pile and started picking detritus off his waistcoat.

Pauline, close behind him, called out: "Vic! Some-one for you!"

While the whole top floor was obviously a single room, as much as a third of the floor space was taken up by a stage, concealed front and sides by a green velvet curtain.

A voice came from behind the curtain, a man's voice with a gritty edge to it and the long trailing 'A's of a Londoner: "Linda! Where's Linda?"

"Not back yet."

"If it's the Mozart fellah, then okay."

"That's the one."

The flat of a hand pressed into the small of Sandy's back just as he himself started to move, ready to rise to the challenge of anyone who would risk the tired schoolyard gag in his hearing.

When he got to the overlap at the centre of the curtains, he pulled the heavy drape to one side, stepped up onto the podium, and let the material fall back behind him. There he paused, precarious on the inside edge of an enclosed stage, needing to hang onto something.

The stage was bathed in a dim orange light and was dominated by an enormous bed that extended across the centre. To Sandy's left a grand piano stood with its lid open, and to his right there was an upright. Beyond that, a sink had been mounted on the back wall and bore the copper-green stains that would be natural if it was plumbed in.

A man with a square face, pointed chin, not much hair and half-moon reading glasses sat on top of the bed in a silver, silk dressing gown, and was propped up by pillows. With a flurry of the stapled sheets of paper he had been reading from, he ushered Sandy to the larger piano. "Let's hear you play."

Three single-sheet pieces were set out neatly on the music rack. Sight-reading, Sandy faced a single melody three times over: once treated simply, once as a jazz piece, and once as a sour, moody violation of standard music progressions.

Was it too much of a risk to give his own, personal rendition of each piece?—to do what in any other circumstance would count as *showing off*. Yet if he was aiming high, if he believed he was capable of working his way up to star billing, he had to have his own voice. He had to rise above the prosaic.

To be *anything* you had to *be* something.

So he set to it.

The melody, he played with humour. The jazz, he mangled into blues. For the sour, moody offering, he remembered a stand-in organist at a rehearsal for a piece composed by the head of his music school. The stand-in had played the music exactly as set down in the score, but had got it all wrong. You had to hear the music in real life to know how to play it. Sandy examined the piece before him. What was the composer trying to do? The emotional truth of it lay beyond the muscular precision of the notes on the page and, in the end, he could only guess. So long as the piece felt like a unified whole, was consistent, and advanced with visceral force and, he might hope, some subtlety...

He played.

Before the last note died, Vic Victor said, "Which do you like best?"

That was not difficult. "The last."

"Why?"

"It holds my interest."

"It says here you act."

Sandy rested his hands on his knees to stop them shaking. "Sure."

Vic Victor turned his head to address the curtain. "Linda? You here?"

The curtains at the end of the bed parted, and the woman in the blue boiler suit stepped up onto the stage carrying a pile of newspapers and the mail.

"A newsreader," Vic Victor said, "reads out a news-flash of a plane crash and realises that his wife is on board. Okay?"

Sandy put his hands to his face, filled his lungs and stiffened his back—how on earth was he going to make this authentic?

He imagined he was on stage in the West End in an experimental performance that mixed fact with fiction. He imagined he had volunteered for the fac-tual role. His job in the production was to read real, live newsfeeds from an autocue in front of a camera. His factual reading would be broadcast live, together, side by side with the on-stage fiction, in split-screen. His imaginary director said, "Be yourself. Speak clearly." Sandy, the newsreader, was not even being called upon to act.

He relaxed before the camera, which he imag-ined next to Vic Victor's face but, by a trick of the low orange lighting, not visible.

Sandy put his finger to his ear, and listened. "We are just receiving reports," he said, "of a plane in dif-ficulty over the Atlantic—" there are planes in diffi-culty all the time, are there not? Bird strikes, lightning strikes, an engine on fire. Plenty of things go wrong, most of them routinely dealt with by professional crews. The words he was speaking were literally true, somewhere. No need at all to act, "—being diverted to Shannon airport."

Sandy sort-of remembered the format of flight numbers, but the question was, how to authentically conjure up a non-existent wife who was on board? Well, there had been that American girlfriend Curtis, the other music scholar at Pemberwell College. They'd been pretty close. But they'd split up when she was forced to go home. It was not beyond possible that she had taken it into her head to come back. Just for him. With one intention only...

And they fly everywhere in The States, don't they? It was not beyond possible that she was in the air at this very moment.

Listening intently to his earpiece, Sandy carefully read out the flight number that was on the ticket on her lap as she sat on the plane.

Then he spoke the phone number that the public should call for more information, desperately trying to memorise each digit as it passed his lips, so he could dial the number himself, as soon as he was off air.

"You sing?" Vic Victor said as soon as the last digit of the phone number had left Sandy's lips.

Remaining in character, staring at Vic Victor and the imaginary camera, Sandy nodded.

"Anything you like," Vic Victor said, but added, "unaccompanied."

This was the one thing Sandy had prepared for. His party piece. The one he used to shock old school friends when they visited him from up north, doubting that he would amount to anything, and anxious to see him fall flat on his face.

Except he was still dazed from his newsreader performance, as if what he had said was actually true.

"Glass of water?" Linda said, putting the pile of newspapers down.

Struggling to find a voice, he had to consciously draw breath to say, "Thanks."

Linda filled a tumbler of water at the sink on the far side of the bed and passed it to him.

"In your own time," Vic Victor said, looking at his watch.

Sandy stood. His throat was still dusty, he'd had no time to warm up, and he'd just bruised every emotional muscle he possessed. How well could he do this?

He called to mind the limp oval face of Gary Palini, the mouthy school bully who had come up to London with the others to see the graduation show that Sandy had penned, expecting—Sandy had no doubt—to see some amateur production and to find ample opportunity to mock.

Mock they did not.

Sandy held Vic Victor's eye and tapped into some of that *I'll show you, you bastard* spirit.

He started to breathe for his song like he was being counted in. With the invisible tuning fork of the mind, he summoned the key, the timbre, and the first note he would deliver to this hostile audience. He willed surprise on the face that challenged him:

"Che bella cosa na jurnata e sole...

He held eye contact, and developed the tune. He rounded on the words with force and precision and poured them out. With some strange mix of lust and anger he modulated the air that he pushed from his lungs and moulded the sounds that issued from his mouth and, with the unstoppable action of a wave as it breaks on the beach, as he came to the end, he knew, he just knew when he reached the chorus of 'O sole mio that he had hit the spot. He had done the best he possibly could. If they really honestly, *honestly* didn't like that, The Musical Theatre Company was not for him.

Shakily, he finished the glass of water and sat down.

Beyond the curtain someone wolf-whistled and there was applause.

Vic Victor said, "You do realise, mister *Amadaay-us*, in this company, everyone turns their hand to everything. No one is special."

"I read that," Sandy said.

"Know what we're working on?"

"Only rumours."

"That's because we're not even past the first cue. What I want, what I need, one month from now, is for you, or Linda, or Pauline or whoever, to be sitting where you are now, with a true story in your hands, explaining to me how it captures the essence of a tragic life. Of love won and lost, of death, perhaps murder, of betrayal, injustice, tragedy and redemption. We will make the audience laugh; we will make the audience cry; we will relieve them of the burden of the daily grind. Take them to a place they have never been before—well at least not since Gaius. How are you, mister *Amadaay-us*, with that?"

"Story maker?" *Know the role, be the part, make it true* had been the mantra of his tutor at Pemberwell, and if Sandy was in on the story—a true story at that—from the start...

"Maker this month," Vic Victor said, "player next, who knows..."

"Absolutely," Sandy said, a little more enthusiastically than he intended. He couldn't help himself. To join the company any way, any how. "Sure! I'd love to." He was shaking his head in appreciative agreement. "In from the start. Absolutely."

"Linda?" Vic Victor glanced towards the curtain. "Envelope."

Linda took an envelope from the top of the pile of newspapers and handed it to Sandy.

"There is a newspaper cutting," she said, "of a story a superfan sent us as a suggested starting point for a real life story. Most likely it will come to nothing, but it will get you off the ground. You never know..."

"Back here nine a.m. tomorrow," Vic Victor said, "and you'll be introduced to the rest of the team. You started working for The Musical Theatre Company forty-five minutes ago. Pay is weekly in arrears for the first two months. Then when we know we're all madly in love with each other, you move onto the permanent payroll. I've ordered some sheet music from Chappell's. You can collect it today. Bring it with you tomorrow. Just say my name."

Sandy took the envelope, his hand trembling.

He parted the curtain and stepped off the stage, realising as he descended the stairs from the top floor that in his haste to make a start, he never said *thank you*.

"What did I tell you?" Linda Turnbull said, after a suitable pause. She was nicely satisfied that Ruby Rattler had yet again come up with the goods, this time in the form of Sandy Amadeus.

"Sure. I'm feeling T-O-L-D," Victor said. "Unless I've just engaged another Barry."

"Without Barry there would have been no Gaius."

Linda was reluctant to stand up for Barry. But when it came to *Gaius*, he had been the heart and soul of the show. There was no denying that. Once you'd seen the man and heard the voice, you couldn't look away. You couldn't bear to hear anyone else in the role. That's what they needed now. Another Barry. Barry's downfall was, well, just bad luck, even if, kind of, foretold. But this Sandy Amadeus, he clearly had something. He just needed shaping.

"Any post?" Victor said.

Linda passed him the accountant's quarterly income report, which was what he was really after.

"Down again." He placed his hands behind his head, leant back and closed his eyes. "I need the next show, like yesterday. Until then, *someone* must know: what can we use eight hundred seats and a stage for?—

and don't you dare say the B word."

Linda believed in The Musical Theatre Company. She believed in Vic Victor junior. She believed in the stage musical as the most magical, most moving expression of the human condition; she was hardly likely to say 'bingo'. Nor was she about to repeat any of the dead-end suggestions she'd heard over recent weeks and months, none of which could busk a dime in the face of MTC's looming crisis.

"Everyone we negotiate with," she said, "arrives at the negotiation either believing we're desperate or believing we're loaded with royalties from Gaius. To a man, they believe they can write their own terms."

"Find the zeitgeist," Victor opened his eyes and levelled his head. "We live in a time of change. We need to tap into that. You're the one with the contacts. All those ears to the ground. Find the tomorrow thing. What about this internet people are raving about? Is that set to be the next big one? Maybe we can do something with that?"

He glanced again at the accountant's report. "Even if this Sandy *Amadaay-us* is the talent we need, it's going to take time. It's a big ask. Even if we hit on the right story, like tomorrow, it's all going to take time. What d'you reckon: is it too soon to tap Joanne for more cash? You tell me, it's your territory. But that'd be useful. Really useful. *Heh!* Perhaps you could ask your Ruby Rattler friend to lend us a few bob. What d'you think?"

Linda switched on her most patronising smile.

"If only Ruby was an angel of the cash-giving kind."

But Ruby Rattler never had been that kind of sponsor. For sure, she was queen of the pre-rumour rumour. She had alerted Linda long in advance to The Templar's Arch Theatre being put up for sale, allowing MTC to get in there first, buy it, and rename it The New Caesar. And Ruby had contrived an informal meeting between Linda and Joanne Cambridge, the entrepreneur, who was now MTC's largest backer. Their most generous angel, by a long way. Whatever their plans, Ruby was always somewhere in the wings, never out of earshot, never too far away to offer a useful prompt. But always keeping to the shadow. More recently, of course, she had pointed Linda in the direction of Sandy Amadeus and his self-penned graduation show. Ruby seemed to belong to some mysterious echelon beyond the reach of the struggling artist. But however she did it, Ruby was a boon to Linda's personal, one-woman campaign to keep MTC afloat: to pay her incalculable debt to Vic Victor senior.

And yet Linda's overture to Ruby always ended on the same off-key note because no one, least of all Linda, had the faintest idea who Ruby Rattler was.

CHAPTER TWO

The man in the elbow-patched tweed at the Grosvenor Street Post Office looked down at Angela through the glass screen and in a squeaky voice said:

"You'll need a big strong bloke to help you with this one, luv."

Angela smiled one of her courteous, *another clueless Englishman* smiles, dragged the cardboard package which was the size of a hat box out through the open hatch and balanced it on her hip. It was indeed heavy, but she was damned if she was going to let it show.

In a hobble and a hop, she turned half circle and started back down the lunchtime queue of those waiting to be served. She held her head high, kept her face forward, and set her eyes on the glass door to the street. The package pinched the skin of her waist and risked stretching the blue fabric of her dress, but she managed to suppress a grimace and resisted the temptation to put it down and walk it across the floor.

This was not what she'd been looking forward to five weeks earlier, when she'd stepped briskly off the plane at Heathrow, bursting with hope and energy. But never mind. It was what she was doing now, and it was only a matter of time before she would hit upon something to set herself back on track. To catch up with destiny.

It seemed that fate demanded that her life move forward through a series of dramatic little epiphanies, good and bad, each crystallizing a peak or trough in her career that demanded she pivot through some dramatic little change. So she knew there was another little pivoting on the way, just around the corner, because there was always something. The important thing was that she recognize each new opportunity for what it was.

As she hobbled along the queue of blank-faced secretaries and dull-eyed office juniors clutching their post with the patience of a stopped clock, it was a mystery to her that any fully conscious soul could put their life, willingly, on pause. They must never have had that exuberant feeling of breakthrough. Of the hope and joy that came with positive change. She had been a mere fifteen years old when she had discovered that. When she was offered a part in a Brazilian soap and, after begging her father, and with the blessing of her mother, and ignoring the condescension of four brothers, she had learned with ecstatic pleasure that the thing that she did which she called *acting* counted as acting to the real adults. Her mother's tearful reading of the letter from *Mídia de Televisão Brasil* to the whole family at breakfast echoed now in her ears, when just ahead of her a flicker in the queue in the post office drew her eye.

A man about her age in a mustard yellow shirt, grey waistcoat, bootlace tie and giggle-worthy ponytail had turned his head and was watching her. The very slight curvature of his lips suggested a smile, but whether he was mocking or sympathetic to the difficulties of a soulmate, she couldn't tell. Normally she would have ignored anything so subtle by way of a greeting—her fan club back home numbered over 300,000 and 'subtle' got lost in the noise.

Yet here he was. He stood out from the queue. He was the only one not imprisoned by some grey office uniform and, what she couldn't avoid, his eyes were dark and alive. It was as if she knew him already, had known him forever, from some shared production a long time ago, in pre-school perhaps, and yet she couldn't rescue his name from memory.

Fascinated, and fully aware of an eerie compulsion, she lacked the will to take her eyes from his face and promptly banged her heavy package into a display case. Fumbling the package, she dislodged several clear-wrapped packs of Sellotape, knocking them across the floor, where they tumbled to a halt by his feet.

She felt the whole queue rotate its stopped-watch stare to bear down upon her with an immobilizing glare.

"I've got them," the man said in easily understandable English.

He squatted and, in a single, sweeping movement, a ballet dancer's movement, scooped up the fallen packets and held them shoulder-high, ready to return to the display.

Curiously fazed, she found herself borne past him

by the momentum of her lop-sided walk, and in her confusion, over whether she knew him or not, she found herself robbed of initiative.

By the time she got to the post office door (which an old woman with a walking stick was holding open), she was desperately trying to think of an excuse not to leave the building.

Still, she shuffled lopsidedly forward like a zombie, past the woman with the stick, completely befuddled and unable to prevent herself from shambling along the pavement to where a red pillar box stood at the junction with Bond Street. Here, she was forced to stop because Franky, whose pitch this was, had moved into her path and was blocking her way. She let the package slip down the side of her leg to the ground and looked back with stupid despair at the reflection of the street in the glass door of the post office.

"What's eating you?" Franky said, hugging a dozen copies of The Big Issue to his chest and leaning forward, creating a sense of intimacy.

Angela prised open her blue, Italian cross-body purse and started poking around vaguely for loose change.

"Nah! Thanks, but no thanks," Franky said. "You already got this Issue's issue."

"Oh, yes," she said absently, unable to drag her thoughts from the post office. "You're having a good day then..."

"The sun shines. It's a good day."

She pulled out a five-pound note. "Here, have this."

"No, no, you can't do that. You earned that. That's yours."

She stared at the wad of The Big Issues he was nursing. "I'll take it out of petty cash. Rupert is always saying he wants the shop for the shop's sake and hang the profit. So I'm only doing what I'm paid to do. Here, I insist."

Franky took the note and half-heartedly offered her a magazine.

Just then a clear English voice said in her ear, "Can I help with the, er, parcel?"

It was the Adonis.

"Oh, ah, no. Thanks," she said.

What the hell did you say that for?

"How far are you going? I can help a little, surely?" He counted out the cover price of The Big Issue from loose change in his pocket, and added, "I'll have one, thanks. It's exactly what I'm looking for."

Angela had time to recover her good sense. "Tamarind," she said. "I'm going to Tamarind. Down there, see? The shop on the left with the white front."

The Adonis lifted the parcel from the ground and weighed it in the air with his hands. "What is it? Machine parts?"

Machine parts? Was that a joke? Machine parts was movie shorthand for machine guns and rocket launchers. Now she couldn't read his face. It must be a joke. Acting all casual, she said, "It'll be some worthless bit of tat, like the rest."

"It's good to enjoy your work," he said.

What did that mean? Was it criticism? Was he lecturing? She didn't know. But he *was* talking to her. "It's not what I'm trained to do."

"Yeah? And what's that?"

"It no longer matters," she said. "I do something else now." But it wasn't what she meant to say. It came out wrong. "I mean," she said, "I finished my first career and I'm starting another." *Mother of Mercy, woman, why can't you speak straight?*

"You've already finished a career? Wow! Way ahead of me. I'm just getting my first toehold."

"I was a child actress," she said. "But I'm going to set up a fashion brand. When I get a sponsor." Although she knew full well who the sponsor must be. She just hadn't figured out how she was going to get the money out of him—or at least, get her own money back.

"London's the place to be," the Adonis said.

They were almost at the shop now.

"You work near here?" she said.

"I have to collect some sheet music from Chappell's. And I needed a stamp, of course. For a postcard. A Gaius postcard. A souvenir of the old show for my mother. To mark the occasion of some work I've picked up."

Angela wanted to touch him. To reach out and run her fingers down his shirt.

Mary, mother of Jesus—say something! "You might come this way again," she said. "For a piano, perhaps..."

"Then I'd be asking you for help," he said. "This where you work?"

"For now."

Angela unlocked the door and held it open.

He squeezed through into the showroom and left the parcel on the floor next to the glass-topped table at the back where she sketched her designs and waited by the phone for a customer.

As he turned to leave, she wanted to explain why the shop was so empty. An empty shop seemed to her like a failure, but when it came to Tamarind, as Rupert had so carefully explained, there must only ever be one item on display because the fewer things on display and the more square feet of empty space, the higher the price tag, and the better the shop would fit in with the rest of Bond Street. It doesn't matter whether we sell anything or not. He had been emphatic. Just make sure the shop looks like it belongs.

After Rupert's speech she felt she risked his displeasure just changing the display each day. But she had to do something, and that morning she had placed a small white vase on a pedestal in the middle of the showroom. Before she had time to explain all these little complexities, the Adonis said:

"I'll be going then."

"Thanks. Drop in, any time." *Please.*

"Sure. See ya."

The door closed on the gap where he'd been standing. The echo of his footsteps died away on the pavement. He merged with the anonymous noise of London.

She hadn't even asked his name.

Angela stowed the package in the back room among the cleaning equipment.

The mention of 'machine parts' troubled her. She couldn't believe the package actually contained 'machine parts' in the Hollywood sense; that would be a little bit too much monsters of Twilight fantasy. She didn't know enough Czech to know that the writing on the package did not say 'machine parts' although she did know the writing was Czech. And it was way too heavy to be superficial tat for the shop. So while the idea was just too absurd, was she reckless in dismissing the possibility altogether? Why instinctively hide the package, if the idea was as easily dispensed with as the Adonis's joke?

If Rupert Malinbrough (which he insisted she pronounce 'May-bee') had moved into the arms trade, it made him far nastier and more dangerous than she had previously thought. It changed the nature of the risk she was taking in trying to get her money back. Suddenly she was no longer risking some humiliating embarrassment if he found out who she was, now she was playing with her life. She would have to stop thinking of him as a con-man. She would have to rethink the whole venture if she was dealing with a gangster who was all 'tooled up' to spill blood.

But no. She refused to believe the cowardly call-me-May-bee Malinbrough was capable of looking someone in the eye and switching them off like a light. For one thing she didn't believe he was smart enough to get away with it, although maybe mister May-bee didn't know that.

In any case, how could she start a fashion brand without money? She would need to fund equipment and material; pay for her own time; fund premises; pay for an outlet. London had plenty of street markets which would do for a start, but everything here, even a pitch for a stall, cost money, and Rupert had cleaned her out.

So no, she would have to go after him unless she found solid evidence that he was something other than the vile coward who had created a fake property portfolio just outside Prague and conned her and dozens of other actors into investing. Only if she found blood on his hands might she possibly, just possibly give up her cause.

Back at her glass table, Angela stared wistfully through the shop window onto Bond Street.

Over the course of fifteen minutes she counted three Diana dresses in the style of Jacques Azagury, and she realised that passers-by in cheap knock-offs were mingling freely with women who wore the real thing. How irritating it must be for those with the original! She wondered at the mindset of the women who accepted these cheap, phony alternatives. Where was the pleasure? It was like cheating in athletics, you might briefly have the attention of the crowd, but it could not be very satisfactory. Not authentic. You were lying to yourself as much as to everyone else. It was depressing to think that the greedy copycats of mass-production found such a ready market.

But it was a question she must address herself. What did she want of her designs? What would count as success? What would it feel like to encounter a knock-off of her own work, to swish past it, fabric brushing against fabric, in the street?

She wondered about the glitz, the extravagance, the show people put on: the gallery opposite, the parfumier to its left, the jewellers to its right. How much was real? How much, like Tamarind, a facade? The real money wasn't *inside* the shops was it? It was outside, walking the streets, availing itself of the treasures like those opposite, having their pick.

Except success, whatever it was, didn't have to be like that. Wasn't that the point? Being successful meant only that you gained autonomy. You ended up with choice. You didn't have to shackle yourself to a man to make a decent home.

Not for the first time, she considered a return to acting. But no. Not after Hollywood. She was so over that.

She turned her attention to the sketches on the table and noticed the light on the answerphone was flashing.

She leaned across to press 'play', and wondered, wholly irrationally, whether it might be the Adonis.

CHAPTER THREE

The town hall clock struck four as Sandy waited for the archivist in the skylighted roof space of Kensington Library on Hornton Street.

The envelope from Linda Turnbull had contained a newspaper clipping and a hand-written note from someone signing herself Ruby Rattler.

The newspaper clipping reported an accident at a local black spot, at the Olympia end of Kensington High Street, close to where Sandy was staying. A joy rider had jumped a red light, crashed into another car, and run off. There was a photo of a gruesome tangle of metal. The driver of the other car had suffered life-changing injuries and the passenger had whiplash and concussion.

Sandy turned the clipping over and found a date: 12th July 1994, making it three years old.

The note from Ruby Rattler was written with a wide-nibbed fountain pen and dark blue ink on a small sheet of thick, blue-tinted paper:

> Attn: Linda Turnbull c/o MTC
> Dearest Linda,
> Car not stolen. Talk to (i) crash victim (ii) owner. I know you're after a story.
> Warmest regards from your biggest fan,
> Ruby Rattler XX

Sandy wasn't sure that this sort of drama could be adapted for the stage. It was a tragedy for the victim, he didn't doubt that for one second. Whose heart did not pump a little less blood when reading anaemic words like 'life-changing'? But Tragedy on-stage needed to mean something to the audience. The setting had to be crafted, characters developed, stakes established, the audience engaged. An accident was an accident: an arbitrary slug of ill-fortune. Had there been the least hint of a dramatic backstory to this incident, surely it would have been reported? Journalists would have leapt at the chance to cry foul. That was headline stuff. Not this clipping. This Ruby Rattler might be the most earnest fan in the world and yet know nothing about story structure, or character development. Seeing, even appreciating, is never the same as doing or making. *Don't muddle the softness of a carpet in the gaps between your toes with the act of weaving*, his tutor at Pemberwell would say.

Sandy's best guess was that this Ruby Rattler hoped to use MTC to settle a grievance. Obviously, he'd been given a token job to keep him out of the way while the grown-ups did the real work. In the dry heat of the roof space, his resolve sharpened. He could do more than that. He would not be dismissed as a mere trainee. He would play a proper role from the very start. As they would find out.

Juliet, the archivist, was coming back.

For a transient moment, as she walked quietly towards him, a beam of sunlight from a skylight engulfed her head. He was struck by how fragile a creature she was, like a fawn, with light brown hair that was very slightly fluffed, and with translucently pale skin, and freckles.

Seconds later, she set down a pile of newspapers on the table and rested a brown folder on top.

"Gazette, Informer, Olympia Times, The Earls Courter and Mercury." Her voice was soft and unhurried.

Not unkindly, Sandy mused that anyone with a voice like hers was bound to end up working this far above street level simply in order to be heard.

"And this," she placed her left hand on the brown folder, showing off a slim gold ring, "is the council's road safety report on the accident, since there have been several at the same junction." She paused and, as if advising a friend, added: "It's a bit of a rat-run. That turning down Warwick Gardens. If you ask me."

"I don't suppose I can take these away, borrow them?"

She pursed her lips and shook her head. "Not from the reference section. You can make copies." She pointed to a large copier in the middle of the room, next to the reception desk. "So long as you don't copy a whole newspaper."

"And that name?" Sandy said. "Ruby Rattler? Does she turn up anywhere?"

"No record of her. Not on the electoral roll. Not indexed in any of our archives. I also tried the directory of actors' names, because it sounds like a stage name, but she's not recorded there."

"Thanks."

Juliet seemed about to return to her work, when she said, "I do hope they do something about that junction. I never liked it myself."

Sandy nodded. But he was already distracted by the question of *Why now?* Why would anyone, why would this Ruby Rattler in particular, wait so long before acting, before trying to make good whatever kind of revenge this was?

He started thumbing through the newspapers, looking for mentions of the crash or the road junction. As his finger tips turned black with newsprint, and his eyes grew blind to patterns of words, it occurred to him that even Vic Victor would have difficulty creating a musical out of such a small, depressing story as this. It simply wasn't big enough to inspire a spectacle. Moreover the mystery remained unsolved. And without a crime and a trial and unless the story already had its place squarely in the public domain, how could they proceed without incurring the wrath of the libel lawyers?

In an hour, Sandy had assembled the following picture of the incident:

At 11:45 p.m. Wednesday 6th January 1993 a car, later reported stolen, and travelling eastbound on Kensington High Street, ran a red light at the junction with the A3220 (Addison Road and Warwick Gardens) and crashed into a car crossing southbound at the time. The driver of the stolen car ran off and was never traced. The driver of the other vehicle ended up confined to a wheelchair.

According to the newspapers, which Sandy had no reason to doubt, the wheelchair-bound man now assembled electronic kits for other disabled people who were unable, themselves, to do the assembly, but needed the gadgets.

Sandy couldn't find any journalists' names against the newspaper articles, although the victim and his carer's names appeared beneath a photograph of the two of them at home. Ben Potter in a wheelchair, with his carer father Stan, posed on their narrow balcony on the fifth floor of Trellick Tower. Ben was celebrating one full month out of hospital. The newspapers would have it that The Tower was of architectural significance and offered stunning views of West London. And while the newspapers painted this as a benefit, to Sandy, the words felt empty and flat.

After making his photocopies and leaving the library, he decided to walk home, which took him across the fateful junction. He saw for himself the wide, open roads with clearly visible traffic lights and good fields of view in all directions. Any picture he might have had of an avoidable accident morphed into one of the consequences of reckless chance-taking.

*   *   *

Jodie, the black Labrador, greeted Sandy when he

let himself in through the front door of the large, detached house close to Olympia.

Copal and Meredith Brunwick, the painter and his sculptress wife were holidaying in Crete, but for the last few years they had rented Sandy an annex on the ground floor, at a nominal rent, and never quite got round to kicking him out. And while it meant he felt forever on the verge of homelessness, so long as he stayed here, he was able to help his mother in Rochdale with her rent.

Jodie settled at Sandy's feet while he read and re-read the photocopies, hoping that something new and momentous would strike him. By the time the clock on the mantelpiece chimed half past six and Jodie placed her head on his lap, asking to be fed, one thing stood out that was not mentioned in the papers and mentioned only in passing in the accident report.

Stan, the father, the passenger in the car, claimed to have seen the hit-and-run driver leave the scene, and gave a description of him to the police. They dismissed this on the grounds of his concussion.

What the father had to say might confirm or refute what Ruby implied in her note: that the car was not stolen; that the owner had been driving and was responsible, and by running away and denying his actions was guilty of any number of serious offences.

How any of this could be presented as a musical, Sandy had no idea.

Troubled as he was by the tragedy of this man who was now confined to a wheelchair, Sandy couldn't help feeling, even though he'd never met the man, the scenario was too intimate and private for Vic Victor's supersize stage show ambitions. However, the over-arching feeling, that wouldn't leave Sandy alone, was the sense that he would be preying on the misery of another human being.

CHAPTER FOUR

"I need to place a few ads, that's all." Moe Stone wedged the phone box door open with his right foot to get some relief from the glass-house miasma of sun-cooked urine.

He rapped the credit indicator on the wall-mounted telephone unit with a knuckle. At the other end of the line *that woman* started conferring with someone, her hand over the mouthpiece, leaving him to listen to the crackle, pop and fizz of the line. He continued to rap the indicator, watching it count down, willing it to stop. His thick black moustache, which was long overdue a trim, brushed the mouthpiece of the handset, making him feel soiled; meanwhile *she* was mumbling on and on, and his phonecard was running out.

Eventually the echoey sound of her office returned.

Without waiting for her to speak, he said, "If you could let me have a fifty, that would cover it. See me right. I'll drop by this afternoon. Easy."

It was four o'clock already but he figured these theatrical types worked long hours and Hoxton Square was only forty minutes by tube—if he could be sure to get his fare reimbursed when he arrived.

"You know. For a local story," he said. He had hoped to speak to Vic Victor in person, but found himself fobbed off with Linda *The Icebox* Turnbull. That told him he was on a sticky wicket. Vic used her as a personal bouncer. She was three inches taller than Moe, and didn't she just know it. She made him feel small every time they met. Moe tried to make it all sound like a done deal: "You know for this book Vic agreed to sponsor. Crime City London. You know. That one. Just for ads in local cafés. The library. The local rags and what-have-yous... just a few quid. No big deal. I could write out the ads by hand if you don't want to pay for printing. But better do it all professional. Put on a good show. That's what it's all about, eh? Get the punters to contribute to the, er, punting. Get 'em involved. Make 'em feel good. Good marketing, that. I'm sure you know what I mean."

There was silence at the other end. Like she was waiting for him to run out of words.

Eventually, she said, "I'm really very sorry," her voice was distant and swamped by the fizz and crackle of the phone-box connection, "but we needed those stories from you—not to put too fine a point on it— some weeks ago and all the research for this magnum opus of yours has not yet produced so much as a whisper of anything remotely usable. You promised when you pitched we could have our pick but there's nothing to pick from..."

"Yeah, yeah, but in real life, you know. It's not like you can commit crime to order just to make a story of it. Vic Victor ain't exactly your Charles Foster Kane. Not yet awhiles. You have to wait. To look and listen. To be alert. And have a nose for it—obviously—you got to have a nose for it. But you want something interesting, special. Well, see, they're not that frequent. A lot of your criminal types are sad desperate people, probably damaged, and they do things unplanned and stupid. But your masterminds, the interesting ones, the ones that'll make a good story, they cover up pretty good. So I need to put out a lot of feelers. More and more feelers. I'm putting myself out there in the world to detect your story—I'm your story antenna you might say. It doesn't cost much, but it does cost some..."

The phone line erupted with crisp packet crackles.

"Come to us with the right story," Linda Turnbull said. "I promise, even the merest hint of a decent..." her words disappeared into a blizzard of noise "...get Vic to read to the end of one side of A4, I promise you'll be paid. But that money has to be earned. Same as we earned it by working our tiny cotton socks off to make a success of Gaius. The theatre-goer pays us for product. Likewise we pay you for product. Honestly Moe, we've not had so much as a whiff of a story from you. You must see that."

Moe poked his head out of the telephone box to get a lungful of air.

Two minutes left.

"Look I'll find something, I promise, only—I need a few quid..."

"What did I say that wasn't clear?"

The line crackled with a dusting of applause. Even the phone was taking her side.

"Okay, fine, fine, you made your point. I'll get back

to you on that. I'm on the case already, must go, take care, see ya!"

He didn't wait for a reply, he ended the call. Dammit—too late! The phonecard had rounded down; he had one minute left for a local call.

He dialled the only other number he knew by heart.

God help me if I get the answerphone.

"Carter P Bressier, agent to the stars. How may I please you today?"

"It's Moe."

"Moe? Moe?—oh, Moe! Look love didn't you get my letter? I don't suppose you did, living in your caravan doodah. I know, I know, you don't get post, you have to collect. But you see love, I had to write, you not having a phone and everything, and well, see, the thing is: I can't do it any more. I just can't do it. It's not you, you understand, it's me. It's my gastric difficulties. I just can't stand all the suspense, you follow? I know, I know, don't tell me. Sign of a good story. Loads of suspense, yes, yes I get that. You've nailed the whole suspense thing, *wunderbar!* But frankly, you and I, love, we've come to the end of the road. You're going to need to find—"

The phone line started beeping and disconnected.

Moe kicked the back wall of the phone box, pulled the dead phone card from the phone card slot, and pushed through the phone box door into the fresh air.

Another great start to another great week, he thought. A passing truck thundered through the emptiness of North Pole Road. He flicked the dead phonecard into a litter bin. It was a toss-up now whether to go back to the canal and his narrowboat or visit the cafés where he'd paid to place an ad in the window. Maybe they'd give him a refund if he took the ads down a few days early. Except, he doubted it. Maybe he should try. Scrape together enough for some bread and some cigs. Yeah, but visiting them at this hour on foot? Half would be closed by the time he got to them. He stood a better chance if he did it first thing tomorrow, get what he could in one sweep.

Besides, wasn't there still small change rattling around in the swear box? And he could go through all his pockets. That usually produced a penny or two. Sod it, this was no life. He had to do something. Change something. Stop the downward spiral. There were lots of things he could do. Why wasn't he doing them? Earning decent money from them? He had loads of skills, in particular of the human psychological kind. He could smell dirt—especially human malfeasance—a mile off. He just didn't happen to be living or mixing near the dirt, or in those circles, any more. Not his fault that, not really.

And now Vic Victor, his old chum Vic Victor, had sacked him! Not even to his face—maybe Vic didn't know? Was that it? Yeah, maybe it was The Old Icebox herself, on her own initiative? He ought to speak to Vic direct. Make sure. Unless Vic already had his Big Story. Could that be it? Or Vic had gone and found himself a new Barry Turtle who would solve all his problems, and didn't need little old Moe Stone?

Or, Barry Turtle was back.

Oooh! Now that would be news. Not just the red-tops. He could go to the Sunday Papers with that. Nice one, that. But a bit of a stretch. No, Moe me old matey, we needs to find us the one big story, the one that everyone wants. If Barry Turtle was back, you'd know already, wouldn't you? Even the freebie newspapers you pick up in the street would be caught up in the publicity: Gaius Gets it Together Again; New Stab for Gaius at New Caesar Theatre; Rubicon Rerun—Read All About It! Et cetera, et cetera, et cetera. Blah, blah, blah—Yeah, sure.

He left Scrubs Lane at the bridge over the canal and turned west into the glare of the sun to walk along the tow path to where his boat was moored.

He should clean himself up anyway. He felt soiled from his five-minute encounter with the phone box. His moustache needed washing, and trimming—and his hair. But he couldn't afford a barber, and every time he tried doing it himself, he ended up looking like a mangy black sheep—well, with dashes of grey that he didn't need reminding of.

A narrow boat was chugging along at walking pace towards him, headed for Central London. The bubble and burble of the diesel engine mildly Doppler-shifted to a lower note as it went past. Behind it, the smoke from a stove trailed on the still air and shortly after he caught the dusty aromatic of burning wood blended with the scent of cooking, of beef stew or dumplings, shepherd's pie or cauliflower cheese, or something rich and homely like that. It put a knot in his stomach.

Sod it all! He'd give his brain cells a whisky-reset tonight. There was something left in the bottle, he was sure. He would bleach some neurons for a clean start tomorrow. Why not?

Empty of thought and feeling, he schlepped onward, around a sweeping bend into the next straight stretch of canal.

Even from a distance it was clear that someone had moored next to him, which he was always a bit wary of. If you made a point of choosing somewhere isolated, why did people insist on joining you?

As he reached his boat and stepped onto the stern, he heard a door on the other boat clang open.

"Excuse me!" a man's voice called out. "Any chance of a hand? Got a bit of an emergency."

CHAPTER FIVE

Come Tuesday morning, Sandy did not doubt that 9 a.m. meant 9 a.m., nor that his fledgling story needed to impress, no matter how uneasy he felt about its reliance on the wheelchair-bound man.

"There's no sign outside," Linda had told him the evening before, when she rang to say the venue had changed. "You'll know it when you smell it."

That could have been more helpful.

Now he scurried along Hanway Street, a jumble-edged alley behind Tottenham Court Road, straining ears, eyes and nose for evidence of The Fitzrovia Pool Room & Breakfast Bar.

But maybe she was right because, up ahead, an extractor flue was billowing steam across the pavement and as he got closer he caught the toasty smells of the kitchen: bacon, eggs, fried bread, and coffee. When he reached the flue and passed through its warm mist, he discovered a black metal spiral of steps which led down to a basement. A sign on a string proclaimed in thick black felt-tip: 'We Never Close.'

Sandy couldn't be sure this was the place but it couldn't hurt to look.

He clanked down the steps, tugged open a door that was wedged ajar with a fire extinguisher, and walked into a cavern of cramped, low arches and tightly bunched, round tables. Small spotlights in the ceiling created circles of light on the tables, forcing everywhere else into shadow. The air was thick with the smell of fried foods, although tainted by a sour residue from the drinking and smoking of the night just gone.

Four pool tables had been crammed into the arches by the rear wall. Vic Victor was lining up a shot while Linda Turnbull stood by, waiting, her face illuminated by reflected light from the green baize.

"If everyone's here," Vic Victor said, keeping his eye line on the table, "we start as soon as I win this game."

Pauline was sitting at one of the round tables, her apple-pink cheeks rendered grey in the reflected light. The man and the woman who had been on the phones in the office sat at another. A third table provided a self-service buffet, with steaming plates of breakfast foods in the spotlight.

Sandy slid into the chair opposite Pauline and placed the music sheets he had collected from Chappell's on the table.

Vic Victor played his shot, laid down his cue, and slipped his black jacket over his black round-necked tee-shirt, both of which shimmered as his body moved, as if themselves alive. "Everyone tuck in," he said, going to the food table. "Linda, whiteboard please." He piled eggs, bacon, toast and mushrooms onto a small plate, which he put down in front of Sandy. "Geoff and Rachel meet Sandy Amadeus.

Sandy Amadeus meet Geoff and Rachel. And Pauline, kiddo. We've got three weeks to get us a story. If we can't come up with one of our own in three weeks, we'll have to hire creative professionals which, believe you me, I will not be happy about. So let's find ourselves a story. Alrightee?"

No one said anything.

Vic Victor put his hand on Sandy's shoulder: "Mister Mozart here, goes first. Get it over with. Plus, we get exposed to some fresh thinking without him having time to tailor what he says to what he thinks we want."

With only a hazy idea of what Vic Victor did want, Sandy made his way to the whiteboard which Linda had wheeled to a nearby arch where it caught the rainbow edge of a spotlight.

Sandy tried to read the faces before him, but they were unreadable, bathed in the ghoulish reflected light from the table tops. "The story I had to work with was a car-crash victim with life-changing injuries, who nobly dedicated his life to helping others like him. But honestly, I'm not sure—"

"Let me stop you there," Vic Victor said. "Rachel, you're next. Sandy, you're the new boy so you don't know. You don't know the history of this—not your fault. We need a story that will be as strong as, or stronger than Gaius. You've seen Gaius haven't you?"

"Five times," Sandy said, relieved to have been interrupted, but unsettled that he had gone so quickly wrong.

"Gaius was written by the conqueror of all things Stage, who went by the name Barry Turtle. But we can't have him. What we are going to do is outperform him when he wrote and performed in Gaius—which yours truly scored. What we want on stage is a hero. A character who is outstanding in every respect. Our gimmick for the show is that the story will be of our time. Contemporary. A true story, like Gaius, based in fact, but belonging to the now. We want all the emotions, of course, of course. But with a larger-than-life personality. Preferably a Julius Caesar, but at the very least a Sweeney Todd. Got that? This car crash thing is random and happened to a normal Joe. His good deed, when he had time on his hands, was what—competing with daytime telly? Sad, but we have to deal with the realities of the stage. Our audience comes to London from all over the country—all over the world—for something special—not for Uncle Normal in Street Normal, in House Normal next door. Okay? Got that? Now eat. Rachel, the whiteboard is yours."

Sandy returned to his table but, instead of eating, he edged the steaming plate of food away with his knuckles. He hardly listened to what Rachel was saying. A voice in his head told him to walk out. They'd given him conflicting advice; to research this story *and* find high drama; what was he meant to do? He had not been listened to. He'd been cut short. And yet he agreed with everything Vic Victor said. Why was it so difficult to take? Why couldn't he put a brave face on it? Treat it as an exercise?

He had to ask himself: was this what he wanted? And yet he ought to give it a shot. See what happens. Try to understand what they're trying to do then make an informed choice. Why should he assume learning was painless? To learn something new maybe he had to unlearn a few sacred cows. Unlearn the simple assumptions one clung to for an easy life. But still, he couldn't rationalise away this feeling of being very, very small, and of no use.

Pauline shuffled her chair around the table, and drew up next to him.

Without taking her eyes off Rachel, she said, "Don't let him get to you, kiddo. Working for him will be the ride of your life, believe me. I've been with him five years—no—more than that. Why do I stay? Curiosity. That's the whole story. Curiosity, kiddo. You've got to hang around, simply got to, to see what happens next. You're in for the ride of your life. Nothing will ever be as interesting again. Or as exciting. And, trust me, he wants you. I heard you sing. He'd have you for that if for nothing else. Eat up now. Grab your free meal, you earned it."

After the team had dispersed to pursue their various stories, Sandy wandered along Tottenham Court Road, gazing into the windows of music shops and computer emporiums. The street was empty and most of the shops were closed even though it was after 10 a.m.

He reached Warren Street Station and turned left along Warren Street, towards Regents Park, to avoid the noise and pollution of the Euston Road. There was scaffolding up the front of one building and, as he passed, there was a bang like a gun shot and the clatter of metal behind him. He turned to find a corrugated iron sheet had fallen from the top of the scaffold stack next to him. It had missed him by no more than a metre.

He stared at the dusty piece of metal, puzzled.

There had been no warning, no shout. Had anyone even noticed? There was no one in the street to come to his rescue. He was entirely alone.

On a bright summer's morning as the city came to noisy life, his life might have been snuffed out, lost in an instant, deprived of consequence. He understood intellectually that he must grab whatever life offered when he could. And while he could not think of any action he might immediately take to benefit from this insight, he understood that what Pauline had said was true. MTC was a great opportunity. One must face new challenges, even create them, to give life meaning. Was that not exactly what the creative life was—a life you created that was uniquely what you were able to do in the world? To exist in sameness is hardly to live at all. He should not feel disheartened; he should feel elevated by the failure of his presentation. If he wasn't failing he wasn't trying hard enough, wasn't that the dictum?

Vic Victor had not vetoed the car crash story, he had merely demanded a shape for it. If that shape were there to be found. Sandy's initial proposal had been superficial. What would you expect after less than a day in the job? Vic Victor wanted a true story, and Sandy believed the whole truth of the crash had yet to be discovered. Indeed, when he looked at it like that, he didn't know who these people were, what their lives were like. What were their aspirations and their setbacks? What made them the people they were? He knew nothing about either the red-light runner or the victim.

Oddly, Sandy found unexpected sympathy with Stan Potter, the father of the victim. The father had spoken out and not been heard. What would that have been like? Especially when it really mattered.

The car had not been stolen. That was the implication. Why was that line not pursued?

What was it Ruby Rattler had suggested? Talk to the victim, then talk to the owner? She knew there was a story, she knew full well there was a story. She was spoon-feeding it to MTC. And to Sandy.

As clear as the gunshot bang at the base of the scaffold tower, everything was being handed to him on a plate.

CHAPTER SIX

"Mister Rupert, he say, please bring box to house. Can lock up shop for rest of day."

Angela played the answerphone message a second time, to make sure. *Bring box to house.* Rupert's housekeeper-cum-childminder, Mary, spoke the words softly and clearly and Angela's heart lifted. It wasn't just that it would break the routine of sitting in the shop sketching notional dresses, waiting for no one to come in to inspect the worthless tat on display. No. This was the opportunity, after weeks of waiting, to get sight of the inside of the man's home.

She hefted the heavy hat-box package from the back room out into the street and to the kerb. Locking the shop door, she glanced towards Oxford Street for a cab. As good fortune would have it someone was being dropped off outside Chappell's. She raised her hand and started waving—even though she had been told the English don't wave at cabs, my dear, they hail them or flag them down.

"Angela!" A crisp, authoritative voice commanded from the other side of the street. "Before you shoot off..."

She stopped her arm mid wave and caught the eye of the impossibly slender Craig Olafsen who, in a sky grey suit and white roll-neck jumper, ducked his head as he stepped through the doorway of Arthur Misco-vitz & Sons, Fine Drawings and Paintings, opposite.

"A minute of your time my dear?"

The cabbie drove past. Angela distinctly heard him complain for her to make up her mind, lady.

She motioned to the box. "I can't leave this."

"Allow me." Craig crossed the street and lifted the box to his shoulder. "There's someone here needs to speak to you—tea and a biscuit for your trouble?"

Angela followed him into the gallery which was showing a retrospective of East End surrealist Jim Warren. She'd seen the collection and could see the appeal of his compositions, but preferred less dark and weighty works. It was as if Warren had possessed some kind of uncanny insight into the tragedy of his own death.

Craig said, "It's all very cloak and dagger." He put down the box. "*Mais un soupçon d'intrigue* nicely sharpens up the day."

Angela settled into one side of the Art Deco love-seat in the middle of the gallery. A small table in the same style sat between her and the main exhibition wall.

"Tea in a tick." Craig disappeared into an alcove from which he called out: "Meet Constable Starkey."

Angela twisted her head the other way and realised that her entrance to the gallery had been observed. A uniformed policeman stepped out from behind a painted folding screen in the corner.

"It's nothing to be worried about," the officer said.

Nonetheless, he wrote down Angela's name, her date of birth, and her address. "Basil Street? Don't know that one. Where's that then?"

"It's behind Harrods," Craig said as he emerged carrying a tea tray.

Angela confirmed the location but felt disinclined to volunteer how she came to be living there.

"And are you the owner of the establishment opposite, the Tamarind place, over there with the fancy vase on display?"

"No, no, I—I don't own anything. If only! Not a penny to my name, not me."

"So who does own the establishment opposite?"

"Oh that's the Rupert I was telling you about—," Craig chipped in as he placed the tea tray on the table, "—Rupert Malinbrough—although he insists on pronouncing it 'May-bee'. Like I said, I think you'll find he doesn't quite have the class he aspires to."

"Is that right, Angela...," the officer read from his notebook, "Mistral?"

Angela confirmed Rupert's ownership, and that Rupert was not in the country at the moment.

The policeman explained that the UK Immigration Service was detaining a Czech citizen who had the street address of the Miscovitz Gallery in his possession, alongside a scribbled note with the name Ulan Mikov. Mister Olafsen here, thought the address might be wrong and Ulan Mikov might be something to do with the establishment opposite.

"His real name, is what I said," Craig said.

But Angela was miles ahead of them. She adopted her blankest face. She concentrated on Craig's pouring of the tea. When the policeman asked the question directly: could the two men be one and the same, she said, "Oh, no, I don't think so. That wouldn't be Rupert's style. He's far too direct. No—," although she realised that if the policeman looked at the box on the floor and saw the Czech label, it wouldn't look good. "—But why, officer, what does the Czech man want?"

"We think he came over to kill this Ulan Mikov. He was caught smuggling a firearm into the country."

Angela shook her head slowly. She was back on the set of the teenage soap, playing the hapless naif. "Who would want to kill Rupert?"

There might be a dozen or more people who would do so without a second thought, but who, she hoped, would not. At least not yet.

"Perhaps, Miss Mistral, you would ask Mister May-bee to visit Portman Square police station when he gets back to London. The Immigration Service is faxing a photograph through later today. Perhaps he will recognise our Czech gunrunner?"

"Of course," Angela said. "It's the least I can do."

The policeman leaned over and took a sip of tea from a cup. "Very good, I'm sure," he said. "You won't forget to tell Mister May-bee now, will you?"

Angela assured him she wouldn't.

"If I were you," Craig said, after the policeman had gone, "I'd be looking for another job. I'm thinking our Mister Malinbrough is not the sort of company you want to be keeping. I always knew he was not what he said. He was just a bit too precious about his name. Like names were to be coveted. Collected and coveted. That's what I think. Quite possibly he's all three men, rolled into one!"

Angela doubted that, although Rupert was indeed Ulan Mikov. She could think of a whole host of reasons—and people to match—who might be after his blood. Most important of all, she needed to make her move first. Her whole life savings—every royalty payment she had ever received—had been invested in six fine country properties near Prague. A unique proposition. She still had the brochure. She had been in love with the idea of her own spa village, a place of health, recovery, happiness and personal growth. Ulan Mikov had as good as dashed that hope across the gargantuan rocks of Hruboskalsko.

He was not even Czech, he was a Serb, dishonourably discharged from the Serbian army, who then proceeded to con his way across Europe. It was he who had sold her the properties, only for her to discover, when she had had enough of Hollywood and decided to revert to something more soul-oriented, that the houses, such as they were, had each been sold fifteen times over, and were in a state of utter disrepair.

Dozens of people were similarly aggrieved and one, like her, had obviously managed to trace Ulan Mikov through his colourful name changes and leap-frog travel arrangements but, unlike her, had come with a gun.

She was here first. She had him in her sights. She was going to get her money back. And while, without the houses, a spa village was no longer an option, fashion had always run a close second, and a brand backed by her own money would allow her to stand on her own two feet and regain some dignity.

Until then she was the actress, and she would make this her finest part. Her glorious swan song. Ulan the conman had never met her, so Rupert could have no idea who she really was.

Today was her big chance. For the first time in five weeks of working for Rupert *May-bee* Malinbrough, she might actually get inside his house.

She allowed herself one biscuit, and she finished her tea.

Craig carried the mystery package to the kerb.

She followed him, thanked him, raised her arm, and hailed a cab.

"Morricone Crescent," she said.

CHAPTER SEVEN

It was 8 p.m. on Friday. The last sunlight of the day clipped the tops of nearby houses while, in the deep shadow beneath the flyover where it crossed Portobello Road, Moe Stone rested his hand on a street bollard to steady himself. A gust of wind made him shiver.

That was the thing about living aboard a narrow boat. Sometimes he got land legs and anything as stable as concrete felt like jelly beneath his feet. He was going to have to sit down if he was to read through his haul.

Fabu, the Malaysian restaurant behind him, had been the last of the places where he'd advertised for personal accounts of local crimes. His haul, exactly one week after placing his first ad a mile away in the café by Latimer Road tube station, came to six sheets of paper of assorted shapes and sizes: one neatly typed, one with a drawing, and one joker had made a collage of words and letters cut out of newspapers, like your clichéd ransom note. In the end, experience told him, presentation made no difference. With all such things: content was king.

He crossed Portobello Road, walked past a soiled mattress that bore the spray-painted words 'GEN-TRIFY THIS!' and followed a path into the small public garden that called itself Portobello Green. Only one of the half dozen benches in the garden was not occupied either by kids smoking weed or by tramps drinking from bottles wrapped in brown paper. He sat down facing the white canopy of the Portobello Green covered market and sorted the sheets of paper by size, the smallest on top.

He felt uncomfortable and exposed in the garden. The image of the tramps behind him refused to let him alone. While they struggled for survival, for food and shelter, and numbed the wretchedness of their lives with alcohol, he struggled to discover a crime that would give him a story while ignoring how close he was to similar wretchedness. Was he really addressing the crisis in his own life properly, responsibly, like the adult he should be, but for fifty years on the planet had managed to avoid? The common sense answer had to be 'no'. He was simply doing what he knew best and was comfortable with, and damn the consequences. It was only a matter of time before he ended up on the other bench, with them. But here and now, in this moment, what else was he to do?

The first note was printed in the uneven letters of a child: 'Somebody STOLE Chewy. Can you get him back please?' A second complained about a spate of bike thefts from the railings in front of a row of houses. A third featured a drawing of a robot-like figure leaning over a box next to a chimney stack which was spouting smoke—presumably indicating a rooftop; the picture was captioned: 'There is an alien live opposite me. He plot invasion of world. There are bees, see. He trains them attack. You come see yourself. He think no one see him on roof. I see him on roof.' There was an address. The fourth was the ransom note which stated simply 'Journalism is dead. The news is fixed. You won't root out non-believers using cheap tricks like this.' The sixth note was typewritten on A4 and was an essay on the causes of crime in today's society and how deterrents were not deterrents and cures were not cures and essentially someone should do something about it... But it was the fifth note that Moe read, and immediately re-read, and which connected to his own inner demon.

The note was hand-written in thick, red pencil on lined paper that had been torn from a spiral-bound pad:

I tell you about big con-man. He live Morriconey Cressent. I tell you if you interest. I tell you when meet. You want big story. I give big story. Bad man he. So we meet in public place. If interest we meet Kensington Market 3pm Saturday. A standings only place. It call Rat Soup. Nice and busy. You no there. You no interest. Is all.

There was only one man Moe knew who lived in Morricone Crescent and that was Harry Dagg. Sir Harry Dagg, the gossip columnist. Sir Harry *Me-I-spend-six-months-of-the-year-in-Monaco* Dagg. The monster who got poor, honest Moe Stone sacked from a national newspaper, barred from Fleet Street, and widely ostracized among his former drinking buddies. Any dirt Moe could get on Harry Dagg, even if it was just that Dagg's same-street neighbours were a bit iffy, well, you never knew where a lead like that might lead. Harry Dagg had blood on his hands, not just the blood from Moe's bloody nose, but it was the matter of Dagg and a missing call-girl that had shafted Moe's career.

The promise of payback, and of a juicy story to boot, rekindled the embers deep in Moe's gut like a shot of cheap whisky.

He smelled a story.

Could this be the turning point? Could this put an end to the downward spiral? What karma, what juju, was afoot?

Had he done his penance for some unwitting crime? Or was it those accidental neighbours on the canal? The couple who had lost their electrics, whom he towed to Bull's Bridge for repairs. Had that tipped some cosmic balance?

It was not just a fridge-freezer full of food that they paid him with, but they covered his fuel and, more importantly, his time. Was it too much to suppose that the universe, after forcing him into hibernation, was calling him to action?

It might be wishful thinking, the invention of a righteous, all-connected world, but 'Dagg's Dirty Secret' would make a great headline. Attract readers. Or, if he sold it to Vic Victor, the musical would be *Gossip!* But he shouldn't get ahead of himself. He had to find the story. And the tip-off was only about a same-street neighbour of Dagg, not the man himself.

Moe stood up and stretched. Light was fast draining from the sky. He still felt a little wobbly, but fortified.

On the nearest bench, a man was hunched over, staring straight at the ground, a pile of bags at his feet.

Moe took the man's hand, which was cold and dusty, and pressed a five-pound note into the palm. He closed the man's fingers around the note so it wouldn't fall out.

The man grunted. His fingers remained locked in their new position

Moe said quietly, "Get yourself something to eat."

As he walked away, he wondered whether he would have done the same if none of the café replies had mentioned Morricone Crescent.

But life was too short for that kind of imponderable. His dominant thought as he walked back along the canal was:

Roll on tomorrow. Roll on 3pm.

CHAPTER EIGHT

The only tall building in the village of Cranshaw, where Sandy grew up, was the church where he played the organ in his teens. Before that, his father had served episodically as the organist, but had died from the side-effects of viral hepatitis after serving Queen and Country in Oman. Sandy was proficient enough at the organ to inherit the role, after which the church served, briefly, as his refuge.

The only other tall buildings he had been exposed to in his youth were the Seven Sisters in the nearby town of Rochdale. But Sandy had never been up one of those twenty-storey blocks and only vaguely recalled them as cliff face constructions, made of layer upon layer of ivory-coloured apartment fronts. Trellick Tower by comparison, as it stood before him now, was slim like a book, although the separate service tower at one end made it look like the spine had become detached.

As for what it would be like inside, the media had conditioned him to think of such places as sink estates, to be entered with trepidation. Once inside this shell of 60's concrete, he could not guess who or what he would discover, especially because one of the people he wanted to talk to was likely doubly confined: to a wheelchair as well as a flat.

The church in Cranshaw had risen from stones

planted in Norman times and was solid enough that it would surely outlast the human race, if not God Himself. But the people who attended it—Sandy supposed like people all over—were transient, and ever-changing, a rough and ready mixture of the good and the bad. His first choir master, Douglas Noon took over teaching Sandy the organ after his father died. Six months later, Noon's replacement, Austin Sievad-Moyne listened just once to Sandy's playing, then promptly barred him from performing at services, confining him instead to pipe-tuning duties.

Pipe-tuning was the worst job Sandy had ever had in his life. It involved worming and snaking through confined spaces in the claustrophobic pipe-room, tapping sliders and valves on organ pipes while the organist tried in grim earnest to deafen you. In addition to which, Sievad-Moyne's playing was clunky and artless, and his voice was a nail-scratch squeak; he was horrible to listen to.

To this day, Sandy had a revulsion of confined spaces. Had his father lived, it would all have been different. But he felt awkward complaining to his mother about her spending every last penny on furthering his music, especially when she resolutely refused to unstamp her edict on what she called 'duty-to-talent'. Yet now that the post office had closed, she had nothing to keep her except her war widow's pension, and that was not what it should have been because his father had died after leaving the army.

Sandy came to the main entrance of Trellick which

was at the foot of the service tower and, doing his best to appear rushed and distracted, followed a local through the security door. He nipped, escaping challenge, into the stairwell, climbed the stairs for the fifth floor, and crossed the walkway to the main building.

Only as he stood on the doormat that stated 'Welcome' did it occur to him that what he was doing was outrageous, callous, and probably illegal. Was it really so important to hear the father's side? To find out if the car had been stolen? Should not the poor family's misery remain private? The facts he was after were facts about the world which he could not undo.

He started to feel shabby and exposed, but before mounting shame forced him to retreat, the door swung open:

"Stan Potter?"

The man in front of Sandy stepped forward, into the doorway, and glowered. "What if it is?"

Sandy rocked back on his heels.

The man was in his fifties and had no hair. His face and neck were spongy and red, and in the same way that some men reek of cigarettes, every aspect of this man emitted heat and rage, ready to lead with a fist at the first wrong word.

"I'm an-um-barrister's clerk," Sandy said, trying to think himself into a role, to make this sound like a routine matter. "Our um-chambers have been commissioned to produce an official report on road traffic accidents at the junction of Kensington High Street and Addison Road over the last five years, and..."

"Better come in hadn't you?"

Sandy followed Stan Potter through a short hall into a reception room. The air in the room was tinged with fumes, as if from a badly maintained oil heater, although there was no such heater or burner in sight. It was as if Stan Potter was emitting the fumes himself.

Sandy said, "I was wondering whether Ben was here and might give, um-evidence, too?"

"Ben's dead," Stan Potter said. "Bastard killed Ben didn't he? Not nabbed him yet have you? No, don't tell me. I know. Too much to expect. You sitting down or what?"

"Thanks." Sandy had been edging towards the door to the balcony to put space between himself and Stan Potter and had almost cleared the sofa.

"Tea? Milk, sugar?"

"No sugar, thanks."

"Sit, if you're going to."

Sandy sank into the sofa. It was a loose and lumpy. "The press said—"

"The press. What do they know?"

Stan Potter's fists were clenched and knuckled against his waist. He was trembling as if it was the most terrible effort to keep them there. "Make shit up, don't they, the press? Saying my boy, my poor dear Ben turned his hand to help the disabled like him. What shite. What utter shite. He always done that, see? Even before. Always. Always helped them people less well off than him. And what that joyriding bastard done. How much damage. How many lives he ruined for his joyriding? Tell me that! You need me to spell it out or what? No way was it stolen. Not that car. I was there, see. I saw the driver. Besides, who'd steal a shitbox like that? Not in Holland fucking Park when you got fucking Ferraris and Lamborghinis and Maseratis—I watch 'em all day, coming and going. Those are the cars to steal—and they do, don't they? Steal 'em to order, they do. Besides, they found the keys in the ignition. And the theft was only reported after the crash. How fucking stupid you think we are? Just 'cos we live here. Stuck up in the sky and forgot. Sure. You gonna do something? Sure. Like hell you will. I won't hold my breath."

Sandy was sinking deeper into the sofa, unable to get up, trapped in the room. He could feel the heat radiate off the man but couldn't look away, couldn't take his eyes off the twitching fists. He knew with horrible certainty that he shared the room with a ticking bomb.

"And them people Ben helped? Landmine victims, they were. Consequences, see. Consequences. You talk to them victims—then you talk to the driver. The one as had his car stolen. See, I know who he is. *Aha!* See. They don't know as I knows that. I'll give you a name. If you want a name. Probably you know already. 'cos no one tells me diddly fucking squat. But I'll tell you who he is. I'll tell you, on condition, on condition you swear your lawyer's oath, you go see him. You put it to him. Put it to him, he was driving. My life savings says

66

he can't look you in the eye and say no to that. You ask him. You want to know what happened. What happened is *he* happened."

Stan Potter had been edging forward and was now leaning directly over Sandy.

Sandy had sunk back, deeper into the sofa, which was slowly giving way beneath him while hot dabs of spittle sprayed his cheeks as the man spat words out.

"I intend to," Sandy said. He had already decided he was never doing anything like this ever again. "Yes. Obviously I need to..." He rolled sideways, levered himself up off the padded sausage of material that did for an armrest and managed to stand.

Stan Potter remained stooped over the sofa, frozen in position, shaking. Tears streamed down his cheeks. Without moving, gasping for air, he said: "Carlos Nix. That's who you want. Carlos Nix, he's the bastard. You put it to him. He killed my son. With his bare hands at the wheel of a car. You put it to him, you promise?"

"I'll put it to him," Sandy said. "I promise."

"Well..." Stan Potter kept his fists piled into his waist as if paralyzed in a spasm of arthritic pain. He continued to speak to the empty sofa. "Sixteen Morricone Crescent. You'll find him. Put it to him. Good and straight. To his face. Put it to him. Put it in your report. Put it in your report, and be sure and tell me."

Sandy wanted to put a hand on the man's shoulder, but couldn't. Not because of the fists, but because of the tears streaming down the man's cheeks.

67

CHAPTER NINE

In the back of the black cab Angela hugged Rupert's package to her stomach and shuffled forward to let herself out.

"Here darling, you want an 'and with that?" the cabbie said.

"No thank you."

It must be the package, she decided. At the airport, with three heavy suitcases, she'd been offered no help at all. Nor when she'd carried an ergonomic chair from Cassway & Coopers in the Kings Road to her room in Basil Street. But a man sees something he can easily carry, without inconveniencing himself, and he is a fountain of generosity.

"Honest, I won't pull nuffinck," the cabbie said. "Only, with all them steps, you'll be lucky to make it to the front door. Should have had it delivered. I'd have had it delivered—and I got me own wheels. Place like that gallery, bound to have couriers, have 'em on tap as it were. They'll be couriering things all over, least ways to your posh bits of town. They should have offered. I'd have offered. No service these days, that's your problem. You wanna go shopping, you wanna go shopping, you wanna enjoy it. You don't wanna be lugging things around—here, have my card. We do 24-hour call-out and we won't rip you off—nor get ourselves lost—not like them minicabs..."

"Thank you, but no."

She paid him, insisting he gave her three pound coins as change from three five-pound notes. Then, after he made a big show of struggling to find the change, muttering about this being his first job of the day, she made a big show of giving him back a single coin. Did she look stupid, or rich, or merely a foreigner who didn't understand the money?

"Ta very much, I'm sure," he said and drove off.

Angela hefted the parcel onto her hip and went up the steps.

18 Morricone Crescent was a large white-stuccoed terraced house with four floors, five if you counted the basement. She imagined you could easily fit two bedrooms on each of the upper floors. Her family back home could have lived very comfortably in a place like this. Although if you had this amount of space you could afford to have a playroom, and a music room, even a games room. If you were wealthy enough, you could live inside a three-dimensional artwork of your own creation, as Dame Paloma Holman-Watt did, in her uniquely surrealist way in Basil Street. You had to do something with your money. And while Angela appreciated the sharp whiteness of the facade in front of her, the spotless windows, and the miniature evergreen topiary in the front garden, she was not a little sickened to think that a large part of this house, by rights, belonged to her.

At the top of the steps, under the portico, she pushed firmly on the old-fashioned doorbell plunger

69

at the side of the door. It did not move. She tried several times, then she tried twisting it, but it wouldn't twist. Only when, having eliminated all other possibilities, she thought to pull it towards her, did it move. Something brassy in the distance chattered into life.

After what must have been a minute of intense listening, there was a scutter of footsteps the other side of the door. A bolt slid, a chain clinked, and the door opened.

A short Filipino woman, Rupert's housekeeper-cum-childminder, stood with one hand resting on the head of a small girl who had Shirley Temple hair and was wearing a yellow smock with a blue puppy-dog cartoon printed on it.

"Hello, you must be Mary," Angela said, then, looking down, "and you must be Tangerine."

Mary said, "You please to come in."

Angela left bright sunlight for cool gloom. She slid the parcel to the polished wood of the hall floor, fished around in her purse and brought something out, concealing it in her fist. She squatted to Tangerine's level, long prepared for this moment.

"No school today?"

Tangerine shook her head.

"I've got something for you. Like to see what it is?"

Tangerine nodded.

Angela opened her hand to reveal a turquoise owl brooch.

Tangerine's mouth opened wide. She fumbled the brooch from the palm of Angela's hand then, alternately holding it at arm's length and clamping it to her pumped-out chest, she wriggled left and right.

"Now *dayong*, what good little girl say?" Mary said.

Tangerine hugged the brooch to her cheek. "Thank you."

"Please bring parcel. Follow me." Mary said. "Unless it too heavy, I think?"

"Don't worry about me," Angela said.

Mary, taking Tangerine by the hand, led Angela through a concealed door under the main stairs onto a wide spiral staircase constructed of glass slabs that led down to the basement. Going as fast as Tangerine's carefully planted feet allowed, the three of them descended into the bowels of the house. As they completed the first half circle of the spiral, and as the daylight from above all but ran out, an array of fluorescent tubes at ceiling height flickered automatically into life.

Angela let out a little *oooh!* of surprise.

The basement was not a basement in any usual sense of the word.

They arrived instead on a glass-floored, glass-walled balcony that encircled an even lower, second basement containing a swimming pool.

They continued all the way down to the level of the pool, and Angela was about to deposit the parcel on the blue and white tiled floor, when Mary indicated a wide opening in the floor in the far corner. "We go one more down."

The final flight of stairs was concrete and the three

of them ended up level with the bottom of the pool where there were pipes and pumps and large plastic barrels of chemicals. There was also a large glass window that allowed anyone down here, below water level, to watch the swimmers. Like a shark tank at a zoo.

It reminded Angela of Hollywood and added an extra, sleazy side to Rupert. She felt a little soiled even knowing about it. "You ever go swimming?" she said.

"Not me." Mary shook her head. "I not swim too good. Enough to get child to edge if accident. But not good. Mister Rupert, he not employ me for swimming. Please to leave parcel here."

Angela put down the parcel.

Tangerine was gazing at the floor of the pool with her nose pressed to the glass.

Dappled patterns of light shifted across the tiles, synchronised with the traffic above and, every few seconds, an extractor fan near by clunked on and off with a distinctive thud, and triggered its own little cross-waves of chaos.

"I can swim," Tangerine said. "I can swim up to my elbows."

"She paddle at the beach," Mary said. "But you not allowed here, are you *dayong*?"

"What's the large round plug in the centre?" Angela said. It was like the circular hatches they love to struggle with in submarine movies. "Surely a pool doesn't have a plug hole?"

"That Mister Rupert big secret," Mary said. "That

his secret he like tell everyone. That his safe. He tell everyone, 'there my safe. Only thing is, won't open unless pool empty. Pool take one hour to empty. In that time, I catch you.' That what he say."

"My real mummy teach me to swim," Tangerine said, talking into the glass, steaming it up with her breath, then wiping it clean with her hand. "That's what mummies do."

Angela hardly heard the child. Those few words, 'I catch you,' wouldn't leave her alone. She felt uncomfortably cold, and had the horrible feeling that getting here had been too easy. As if Rupert knew all about her and was taunting her. Or had he set a trap and she had happily marched into a gilded cage? But how could he know who she was? All their financial transactions had been, quite deliberately, through third parties, through properly constituted advisers so she didn't get ripped off. Supposedly. Her worry about being exposed passed, but her sense of unease lingered, and she decided that being this far underground with only one way out was not the best place to be.

Tangerine was saying, "My mummy she had to stay there. Daddy say I get new mummy soon. She teach me to swim."

"What's in the parcel?" Angela said. "Since I carried it all this way, I'd like to know."

"Oh that? It new pump." Mary pointed to a large pipe that ran at head height parallel to the viewing window. "See?"

There was a bucket under the pipe where it joined a metal doughnut.

"Old pump, it leak." Mary said. "I change bucket three times a day. Mister Rupert, he say, dammit and get all new. Don't piss about. That what he say."

Don't piss about. Yes, Angela couldn't agree more. She was much closer to her goal, that was the main thing. And soon, one way or another, as soon as she could, she would take resolute action. Although exactly what action, she had yet to decide.

CHAPTER TEN

"I'm very sorry mister Cramptin," Linda said. "We're not recruiting at the moment."

She was sitting behind the desk in her office backstage at the New Caesar Theatre. The man in front of her was in his early thirties, with a crew cut and in magenta jeans. He wore a dark green jacket over a zebra-stripe tee-shirt but somehow, through the way he stood and the cut of his clothes, he achieved the surprising, unexpected elegance of an angelfish.

"We don't recruit between productions." Linda parted her empty hands to emphasize she was powerless. "It's management policy." Not to mention that, these days, three or four people a week came in off the street looking for work and must be turned down.

"Call me Crispin, *please*. Look, see, the thing is: Ruby Rattler said to talk to you. In point of fact, she said I should be specific and mention her. And—look here now, let me be straight with you—she said her contribution to MTC meant her credit with you was good. So it would be productive for me to ask. 'Timely' was the word she used—were you to twist my arm et cetera, et cetera and demand God's honest truth."

Linda half-listened. In a world where everybody claimed to know everybody he'd done his research and obviously read the infamous story in the music press about the mysterious Rap Banter superfan. He was not the first to try that. But he needed to do more than mention Ruby to convince Linda of his bona fides. Sadly for him, as soon as Linda heard anyone profess to speak the honest truth she assumed she was hearing anything but. And Ruby Rattler had only to drop Linda a line so, no, she didn't believe this man any more than if he'd claimed to have gone to school with the Princess of Wales, been the godson of Neil Armstrong, or had a bit part in Star Wars. How many people ever presented themselves at interview claiming to be a nobody? Nobody was a nobody, that's how many.

Through the glass in her office window, which overlooked the main access corridor backstage, a grim-faced man in a removals uniform and a flat cap was wheeling off to auction the last of the pop-up desert cacti from the long-dismantled stage set of Gaius. Five thirty on a Friday, the removal men were running late, and she might have to start paying overtime to the stage door keeper.

"And just how do you come to know Ruby Rattler?" Linda was vaguely curious as to how far down the rabbit hole this fabrication might go. Her expectation of getting closer to Ruby Rattler through Crispin Cramptin remained resolutely at zero.

"I know lots of people," Cramptin said. "I know that Barry Turtle too. Known him years. Long before the, well, you know, fame."

She couldn't fault the guy for trying. Maybe he did

know Barry, maybe he didn't. His CV claimed he'd been working as an interior designer for names she recognised from the newspapers. Quite possibly he'd bumped into Barry at some party. Cramptin certainly looked the part. He had a presence, she couldn't fault him on impact. Any man who could pull off the combination of magenta, green and zebra stripes—well! There was a hunger about him too. Though hungry for what she couldn't quite say. Whatever it was, she sensed he had a voracious appetite whenever he stumbled across his personal brand of ambrosia.

Sad for him though, despite what the press had said about Barry and her, that was the one name Crispin Cramptin was ill-advised to drop. Not after what Barry had done to MTC, and to *Gaius*—and the forever declining prospects of the New Caesar Theatre.

Although, if he had plausibly met Barry, could this man also know Ruby Rattler?

"I saw you perform," he said.

"You're not that old."

"No. Honest. I did. I loved the stage set. Hammersmith Odeon, 1985. 'Go Go Go Say-Ya-Mean Wo Wo Wo!' Brilliant. Don't know why you broke up."

"Bands do," she said. "The music business is more fluid than people think. Everyone wants stability in their stars. They want immutable idols. 'How like a god.' But sadly we lack the permanence of gods. We all grow up—well, most of us do."

"Hamlet quotations aside, I saw you in Berlin, too," he said. "And Singapore."

"What were you doing in Singapore?"

He smiled like a child charming his way out of trouble. "Bit of a Banter groupie me, in my youth."

"We're all entitled to a youth, Crispin," Linda said, offering him back his CV. "The trick is not inhabiting it forever."

He ignored the CV, which hung in the air between them. He said, "I have worked in the theatre before. That is to say: once."

"You don't mention it." She withdrew the CV and checked it.

"I was a stage manager at the Young Vic for my gap year. I designed the implied cellar for the 360 degree stage in their Cask of Amontillado. The set design won an award. I was part of that."

"Really? I saw that show," Linda said. "Why did you leave it off your CV?"

She checked the CV again, this time running her finger down the entries, looking for anything that sounded theatrical.

"Besides," she continued, "that places you at college in the early 80s. What did you do between college and '88 when you were working in interior design? How come you've grown five years older in as many minutes?"

"Oh my god. Found out!" He raised his hands in surrender. "Well, I was doing fashion for a multi-national. But people don't always like cross-over designers as it were—I mean, from fashion to theatre, or vice versa."

"Why would you think that?"

"You lack commitment. Go from theatre to fashion and you're chasing spondulix. Go from fashion to theatre and you're getting above yourself. Either way you're not taking your pain, serving your apprenticeship like the rest of the gang. You're always the opportunist and interloper, looking for short-cuts. And the obstacles the time-servers put in your way, not nice... But, the thing is, now you found me out, let me be honest: I designed everything on the *Cowbart Casuals* clothes label for their *Red Vector* brand of denimwear. That was me. My encounter with fashion-biz. You could use that in your publicity." He made air-quotes: "Cowbart Casuals Designer Sires Stage Set Successor to Gaius."

Linda studied his face, now seriously trying to place him. She had seen him before, of course she had. He'd been in the magazines. He'd even been mooted briefly for the Diana wedding dress. "Oh," she said, "you're *that* Crispin Cramptin."

How could she have been so thick? The man had been a brand in his own right. She had simply not made the connection.

She said, "You're saying we could use your name in that context?"

"Absolument ma chérie."

Would Vic buy this? She couldn't see why not. The man's name would bring a demographic they sorely needed to tap into. But why hadn't Crispin Cramptin mentioned it before? Why hide it? Age-vanity? And now he was doing interior design...

She glanced at the clock. Checked for activity on the other side of the window.

Sod it, she'd just make the decision, worry about Vic later.

"I'll tell you what, Crispin," she said. "The idea of a named designer designing our sets appeals to me. I won't give you a prop man position. In the circumstances, that's demeaning. But I will put you on a retainer. We wouldn't want you working for any other theatre company, otherwise it rather spoils the exclusivity. By all means continue with interior design, or clothes design. We'd just want exclusivity on the stage work. How does that sound?"

"How much of a retainer?"

Outside her office, another cactus left the building.

"Two hundred and fifty a month," she said.

"Three hundred."

"Two seventy-five."

"Done."

"You still haven't told me how you know Ruby Rattler."

"I met her at one of your gigs."

Linda wasn't sure now whether to believe him or not. He was hardly the usual man off the street. But if they were working together, she was going to find out, one way or another.

*   *   *

After Crispin Cramptin had gone, Linda wondered whether maybe she had overreached her authority. Was Vic going to see 275-a-month differently? Yet he was the one who said they should look for commercial opportunity where others saw only cheapening of their art. *Advance your art anyway you can. The striving for artistic expression is the life force in us all.* He preached it often enough. *In the private sector we all know where we stand—with less of a foothold than Long John Silver, so grab every opportunity you can.*

There was a knock on the door. The face of Greyhound Joe, the stage door keeper, appeared in the window.

"Come in Grey!"

"'scuse us Miss Turnbull," he said, hardly looking at her.

"What can I do for you today?"

"Well, miss, see, it's embarrassing really. I don't know who to turn to."

"Spit it out. You can't hurt me with words."

"It's difficult, see. I'm a bit behind with my rent. Quite a bit. Everything being so tight these days. And I was wondering whether I could, like, have an advance. You know like a couple of weeks in advance."

"Sit down a minute," Linda said. "Take the weight off."

Greyhound Joe wasn't called Greyhound Joe for nothing. He was a bit too fond of the dogs. He sat down, clutching and wringing his hands. She hated to see him do that.

She said. "How's Betty?"

"Oh, she's doing fine, Miss Turnbull. She's doing fine. Working at Movie Megaplex these days, you know the new one by Leicester Square. Nice bunch of people. But the pay, you know, it makes things difficult. And I haven't had, you know, any more money, since Gaius closed. Know what I'm saying?"

Linda knew what he was saying. She also knew what behind with the rent meant. It meant the last two wage packets had reached the bookies before they reached the landlord. Whatever she paid him now was going to go the same way. Debt only ever ratcheted in one direction.

"Tell you what I'll do," she said. "I'll take your rent out of your wages and TMC will pay your landlord directly, two weeks in advance, how does that sound?"

Greyhound looked puzzled and a little downcast. He said, "Well I suppose, yes that would solve the, er, immediate, um, difficulty, thank you. I'll tell the missus. It will be a load off her mind, I can tell you. Thank you miss Turnbull, you always been good and thoughtful when it come to me and, yes, the missus."

He left, hardly less despondent than when he came in. But the guy was essentially decent and Linda wanted to do the right thing. She had no idea what his life was like, and what she might do in his shoes.

Another thing she should probably have run past Vic; there was an awkward meeting to come.

How does a company go broke? She mused. One penny at a time—wasn't that the saying? Something like that. Besides, how could she criticise the man for gambling? TMC was itself doing just that, hoping to create the Next Big Thing out of thin air. The son of *Gaius*. Hoping to save a whole branch of the theatrical family, The New Caesar Theatre—Linda's people—to avoid it going dark forever. Vic was betting big on The One Big Idea, and he didn't even know what it was yet.

CHAPTER ELEVEN

At 3 p.m. on Saturday afternoon in Kensington Market, Moe Stone could hardly see two feet ahead. It wasn't that everyone was taller than him, though many were, but even those that weren't seemed to have modelled their hair on the wildest bramble they could find, and dyed it black. Walking about in public with hair like that extended the volume of space a body claimed by uncountable inches. Several times Moe was reminded that getting unwanted hair in your face was not only irritating but also, like the tramp's hand, made him want to lather off a layer of dirt.

He pulled his jacket tight. That was the other thing: you could never tell which of today's youth belonged to the criminal classes. On his journalistic assignments he always knew from where he was travelling to, what sort of people to expect. Here, they all wore some variation of the same incomprehensible black uniform with the obvious intention of confronting norms. *En masse* it seemed to defeat the point. He'd only been to Kensington Market twice before, once out of curiosity and once tailing someone who had promptly given him the slip. Had he had a choice he wouldn't have come here now.

He understood from a stallholder at the front that Rat Soup was at the back. By the time he got to the counter—if a plank of wood nailed onto a half-height partition deserved to be called a counter—he was already five minutes late. There were two stools, both taken, so he stood and waited to be served,

No one in sight looked like his informer, although he wasn't sure what to expect. It could be a little old lady with a grudge against one of Harry Dagg's neighbours. Likely she would accuse some ghastly missus Beasely of poisoning Kitty. That would probably be it. Morricone Crescent would be a hot bed of curtain-twitchers and over-the-wall twig snippers. That after all was Dagg's profession. Curtain Twitcher General. Except, what little old lady would arrange to meet in Kensington Market? One with sharp elbows, that was for sure.

Someone behind him muttered, "—if it wasn't for grandad here..." Goddam, Moe, you were just too keen when you saw the street name. He felt trapped and irritated, but his frustration was ill-defined and lacked focus: was it the people, the place, the absent informer, his time-keeping or simply him and his predicament? Sadly, the question actually needed no asking, not really: *Moe, me old matey, Moe—Just how desperate are you?* Just desperate. That's all that's needed isn't it? Just desperate. Desperate for something, for anything to change.

He removed his hat—the one he had chosen to look the part of the detective so his informant would recognise him. It was a half-baked gimmick. He stood out enough anyway.

"Tea, please," he said.

"Camomile, peppermint, ginger, ginseng or black-currant?"

"Builder's."

The black panda eyes of the goth woman who served him seemed, briefly, to go dead. "Like a fairy cake too?" She said.

"No but if you have a builder's, you know. I need the caffeine hit."

"One caffeine hit coming up," she said. "I'd refuse to serve you, normally, you realise that, but at least you bothered with a half-decent hat."

He offered to pay with his last twenty-pound note.

"I can't change that," the goth said. "Sure you won't have a cake?"

"I'm meeting someone, maybe then."

"So pay me when you leave. You can't exactly run away."

She reached for the top shelf and teased a red and white carton of PG Tips into her hand.

As she turned up the throttle on her hot water urn, the person sitting at the counter within nudging distance of Moe's shoulder, left. Moe quickly hoisted himself onto the stool to get a better view.

It was ten past three.

Normally people-watching would engage him for hours, but in the market he was conspicuous and ill at ease. If anything, he was the one being watched. Discretion was not his to enjoy. A few tourists joined and left the throng, venturing as far as the back of the market. They bore the usual trappings: cameras, London landmark picture-bags, and Union Jack policeman's helmets. At one point a man with a small girl riding his shoulders appeared to do one full circuit of the place. Moe guessed it was a full circuit because the girl, who had Shirley Temple hair, was visible above all the goth heads and came up this side of the market, went round the bend, and didn't come back. Moe took the man to be a local because he wore a white blazer with black trim and a gold and red crest. Presumably he was braving the market for the sake of the child. He didn't look too cheerful. His face was lopsided as it was, as if someone had given him a right hook and permanently dislodged his jaw to one side. He was thickset though, and much taller than Moe and Moe would not risk delivering such a punch himself. Moe guessed that the man was a local. He had money written all over him. Although there was something about him, he was perhaps a little too brash to properly belong here. They didn't make a second circuit, so either the girl was satisfied or the man had had enough. Other than the one small incongruity as Moe waited, no one else stood out.

And no one approached him.

It was nearly three forty and he was trying to make a second builder's tea last when he felt forced to conclude this was a no-show. Too bad. It had cost him two cups of tea he would rather not have bought and which he needed now, rather uncomfortably, to see the back of.

Still he must remain positive. He had explored one avenue and come to a dead end. Nipped it in the bud for the price of two cups of tea. That was something, surely. And maybe there was a message here: he should forget Harry Dagg. Moe should instead get on with his life, ditch the past. If he found the right story he had no doubt Vic Victor would buy. The successor to *Gaius* was sorely needed. And he knew pretty much what Vic was after. Only problem was: it had to be a true story. There was even Crime City London. If he could get a few chapters of that off the ground, he knew a few publishers who might go for it. Illustrated it would make a great coffee table book. Hardback and with a strictly functional dust jacket, it would serve as a reference for universities and police forces everywhere. One text, two markets. *Yo Moe!* that would be a neat pitch.

The goth tea lady had been doing a fair trade while Moe had been waiting.

After she gave some small change to the present customer, he said, "I expect you can change a twenty now. What do I owe you?"

"Call it a fiver."

"Five pounds?"

"Your seat-warming deprived me of trade."

In this crowd, Moe didn't feel confident enough to argue. Two cups of tea was one price to pay, but the price of two cups of tea! It was more than time to leave. He reached into his jacket for his wallet.

It was no longer there.

CHAPTER TWELVE

Sandy walked up the steps out of Notting Hill Gate station just over an hour after the team's Monday morning meeting. He headed for Morricone Crescent, feeling unsettled.

He couldn't rid himself of the image of the trembling Stan Potter even though a full week of hectic work at MTC had passed, during which he had helped to research and plot stories that needed more urgent attention than his.

At college, he had learned and experimented with all sorts of creative techniques, from writing down your dreams, to the Cut-up Technique of the surrealists, but nowhere had he come across the method of MTC which, given that even true stories had to be shaped and framed for the stage, was the brutal antithesis of any creative free-thinking process he had ever known. At MTC the idea was to create so much pressure in terms of time and money that you had to grab the first idea that came to mind, run with it until it failed, and then grab another, with as little thought as possible in between. It was like jumping from the top of a burning building without knowing where the air bags were, and repeating the process until you found one.

At that morning's meeting in Hoxton Square, just two weeks into his job, he had heard Pauline recount a diamond robbery motivated by an adulterer's revenge, Geoff recount a bank brought to its knees by a disgruntled employee, and Rachel the saga of an antiques dealer who had fled the family nest after unwittingly selling a forged vase to a Russian gangster. Sandy mumbled something about still investigating and helping the others and was, thankfully, let off the hook. With one proviso.

At the end Vic invoked *Gaius*. "Create a hero for me," he said. "What's so incontrovertibly heroic about any of the characters any of you has brought to the meeting today?"

Vic said he'd commit a crime himself, if he knew how, to give them all something decent, sophisticated, and entertaining to write about. "If it was the last thing I did," he said, "I would do that for you." Which automatically generated an ideal motivation: "A desperate need to create the highest form of art—see, how heroic is that? Murder for your art, or die for it. So long as you make your art big enough. Make sure it matters. Connect it to enough real people and *voila!* They win or lose as your character wins or loses. Now go out into the world and get me that story!"

Sandy walked the streets of Notting Hill. Now that the team had prevailed upon him to see his story through, he had to wonder by what convoluted route his investigation of a road traffic accident was going to produce one such hero. The press tried making a hero of Ben Potter, and failed. Weren't they the professionals at crafting real life into story form? What hope did he have to do better?

A simple childish shame came over him when he thought back to his interview with the garage forecourt attendant who had just lost his son. In retrospect, the whole thing was profoundly distasteful. What had he been thinking? Stan Potter's justifiable rage still rang in his ears and Sandy had to wonder whether he was walking into a repeat performance with this Carlos Nix. Hadn't he stirred it up enough? He cursed himself for promising to put that one question to Carlos. And for acquiescing, just over an hour ago, to the expectations of the team, *and Vic's Method*. And if he didn't believe what Carlos said, what then? For sure, Carlos was not going to admit to manslaughter. Sandy started to think the whole thing was a really bad idea. No one was holding a gun to his head to keep his promise. What kind of weak-minded fool was he?

And yet he remembered what Pauline had said, the ride of his life, and if he wanted to learn, and how hungry was he for success, and if he didn't push at the limits, he would always be limited. But when was it the right thing to do and when not?

He arrived at one end of Morricone Crescent, found number two and started counting. He would play it by ear, he decided. He would wing it. Try to use his judgment. Even if sometimes it was no more than a guess.

16 Morricone Crescent was a white stuccoed house with a squeezed, space-starved London terrace look to it, a little narrower than 18, but the same width as 14.

At the top of the steps, under the portico, Sandy found a door buzzer and a post-it note instructing that mail for the basement belonged down the steps at the side.

He pressed the buzzer, which sounded inside, and he waited.

No one came.

He tried a second time, listening carefully for the least sound inside.

Nothing.

The only sound, apart from the odd car or van driving by, was some trippy Reggae music coming from the flat below.

He made his way down the steps at the side, and tried the basement doorbell. Hearing nothing chime or buzz and doubting any doorbell could be heard above the music, he banged the brass door-knocker.

Shortly, the door cracked open.

"Yeah, you want something?"

Sandy couldn't see the face in the shadow, he said, "I'm new to the neighbourhood. I thought I'd introduce myself. I—er—I volunteered for Neighbourhood Watch and I'm just doing the rounds. Showing my face, and, you know..."

After a pause the door drifted shut, the chain rattled free, and the door re-opened, this time to its full extent, accompanied by clouds of dope smoke, making Sandy's lungs itch and which his voice could do without.

"Oh, yeah, neighbour, yeah, right, come in."

The man had short greased-back blond hair and a beard. Sandy reckoned he was about twenty five.

"Want some?" The man offered Sandy a drag on his joint.

"No thanks."

Sandy was led into the front room which was dim despite the large floor to ceiling window at the front. There were four easy chairs marking the corners of a very precise square that followed clearly-marked light-coloured lines on the carpet. An Asian guy, probably about forty, was sitting in the far chair, rolling another joint.

The music, which Sandy didn't recognise, was coming from two stacks of KEF speakers driven by a Marantz amplifier. He couldn't see the turntable. He guessed these guys were serious about the quality of their music, if nothing else.

"Yeah, right, take a seat, man. Chill. Neighbourhood watch, you say? Someone been complaining? Thought we were over with that. Long in the past, yeah? Here, take a seat, take a seat."

The true walls and ceiling of the flat were concealed under wood-chip wallpaper, and the overall tone was a dull yellow. Probably once it had been white, or cream, but cigarette smoke and London pollution had taken its toll. There were some posters, in odd positions, of Hendrix and Clapton and Che, which Sandy guessed were strategically placed to cover up gaps in the wallpaper.

He settled into the seat offered. He might get

something about the people upstairs. At least he could claim he had tried. Although just being in the room could turn into an ordeal. The fug of hot, tired, smokey air was suffocating, and already his eyes had started to itch.

Thinking to keep this as brief as possible, he said, "You live here?"

"No, man, no. Who'd live here. Like this? Think I'm crazy?"

The Asian man licked the edge of the joint he was rolling.

The blond man continued, "No not me, man I live upstairs. Just come here where I got my sound system set up, and like won't get disturbed. Except by neighbourhood watch. So, anyway, who's been complaining?"

"No one." Sandy placed his hands on the arms of the chair and squeezed the material, wondering whether, if he had to get out quickly, he could drag himself up without difficulty. "I'm just making my face familiar. You know. Getting to know the people. See what crimes, you know, petty crimes, are committed but go unreported because people can't be bothered with the police. That sort of thing."

"You mean, like, this stuff?" The blond man held the joint up, examining it against the light coming from the window.

"I don't think that counts," Sandy said. "Not hereabouts. But bike theft, car theft, even, for instance, I mean—" Sandy shrugged, "—do you drive?"

"Me, oh yeah, I got a nice little runabout, Nice motor isn't it, Si?—Simon here he don't talk much, mainly, you know, chills. Know what I mean? Heh, Si, can we have some different music? I'm bored with this."

Simon didn't move.

"I didn't catch your name," Sandy said.

"Oh, yeah, it's Carlos, I'm Carlos, but everyone calls me Carl, like Marx." He started to giggle.

"You ever had your car stolen?" Sandy said.

"Me? No. Never. See I got a trick. We got a trick, haven't we Si? I got a dead switch, see. Always done that. If you don't know about the dead switch the car won't start. Always done that. Isn't that so Si?"

Simon took a drag on the fresh joint and said, "You're not with the pigs are you?"

"Neighbourhood watch," Sandy said, suddenly alarmed that he didn't even have to ask his question. He just had to get out, with plausible dignity. "Mainly burglaries, that sort of thing. Prevention mainly."

"There's always someone here," Carlos said, "down here, to dissuade them."

"What's the story with this place?" Sandy said, trying to keep the conversation away from cars. "No one minds you coming down here?"

"Guy who lived here," Carlos said, "disappeared. He was a bit of a nutter anyway, you know. Kind of fruitcake. Bit oversensitive. He didn't like music. Imagine. He complained."

"So we gave him some anyway," Simon said, taking a drag. "Like desensitisation. Help him out, you know."

"He was an artist. Artistic temperament an all that. Look at the floor. What d'you see?"

"A square," Sandy said, looking at the lines between the four chairs where the carpet had obviously been compressed and was lighter in colour—and less dirty—than elsewhere.

"Right. Guy had an installation here. Right here in his living room. How nuts is that?"

"Had to be a nutter," Simon said.

"Almost filled the room, didn't it? You could get inside. You saw him inside, didn't you, Si?"

"He had a glass door at the front. Used to look out. Hamster-man, him. Fucking hamster-man. Pratt."

"But he's not here now?"

"Left, didn't he?" Carlos said. "No one knows where to, but the guy who owns the building has a key and asked me to keep an eye on it. You know. Stop squatters. Same as you're doing, in fact. Perhaps I should join Neighbourhood watch. Got their number, have you?"

"How long's he been gone, this nutter?"

Carlos and Simon exchanged looks. Simon shrugged. Carlos said, "Eighteen months maybe. Maybe more."

"Lucky you," Sandy said.

"Keeps upstairs, you know, smoke free."

"Well, it's been nice meeting you." Sandy heaved

himself out of the chair and offered his hand. "Nice to know the building is in safe keeping."

"Yeah. See ya."

Sandy let himself out into the fresh air.

The door clunked shut behind him.

He had to steady himself on the handrail as he struggled up the steps to street level. Every step he went up added a new direction to his dizziness. His stomach told him he was going to be sick. Some logic somewhere advised him of the need to sit down and clear his airways. He couldn't think where the nearest park was. Maybe a café in Portobello Road would do the trick. Some strong coffee, at least. Something doughy to quell his stomach. He reached pavement level, turned left in a whirlwind of slow motion, and started walking carefully and deliberately, taking in deep breaths of air.

A few doors along, a man stepped out from behind some dustbins and, standing directly in Sandy's path, put a hand out to stop him. Sandy worried as he came to a halt that he was going to fall over.

The man was Stan Potter, radiating anger.

Sandy wanted to laugh. He wanted to be sick. He could feel his face creasing up. Bizarrely he thought: maybe this is what it's like to be Stan Potter—you couldn't know could you?

"Okay mister barrister's clerk, what did he say?"

Sandy's head was close to empty of words. Then: "Coffee. I'm going for coffee."

"Yeah? That's nice. My lunch break too. Think I'll

join you." Given the spasms of muscular restraint on his face, Stan Potter might have added, *And then I'll punch your lights out.*

"How did you..?" Sandy said, placing his hand on someone's front garden wall. "How come...?"

"Not so smart, eh, mister barrister's clerk? Not so smart at all. I work round the corner see. I work at the garage round the corner. And when I see you walking by, well, I'm thinking, there's a funny thing. There's a funny thing indeed."

The two of them were close enough for Sandy to feel the heat coming off the spongy red flesh of the man's face. Second hand petrol fumes filled Sandy's lungs. Everything was geared to making his head spin. Mostly though, he was aware of the anger in front of him, raw and untamed, determined and wound up. A ball of wild rage.

He half-sat on the wall and drew deep, purposeful breaths, unable to concentrate.

"And before I let you tuck into your lunch, mister barrister's clerk, you are going to tell me exactly what the bastard said."

CHAPTER THIRTEEN

"You can come back any time you like dear. Don't you worry." The elderly lady put down her black Aynsley teacup (the one with the pink rose pattern on the inside) and she placed a warm hand on Angela's knee, and squeezed.

I can come back, Angela thought, but I hope it won't be in a coffin, or in tins of cat food.

The old lady continued: "Please don't be offended if I don't ask what you are up to. I think I have guessed much of it. My assumption is that we are both better off with my guesses than with the vulgarity of an exchange of concrete information. But, my dear, if your plan fails, please continue to think of my home as a refuge."

To call the house a refuge was something of an understatement.

All the downstairs windows were fronted by steel bars. All the upstairs windows protected by sliding grille gates. There were independent burglar alarms on each floor—independent from each other and from the mains electricity—and there were her modern oubliettes, as Dame Paloma Holman-Watt liked to call them, which would turn any of the exits from the building into miniature prisons should anything move through them once an alarm was triggered.

Each was equipped, of course, with its own little fire sprinkler—one wouldn't want any burglar caught in the act to be fried by the house before he could be fried by the local magistrate.

Any burglar, of course, before anything else, would first face the problem of the mirror house.

Dame Paloma owned not just the one property behind Harrods, but two, knocked together, joined at all levels. And all the artworks she possessed were doubled, throughout the two houses. The original assigned to one house, the best copy that money could buy to the other—both equally secure, and randomly assigned to one or other side of the mirror.

Her little Dodgsonian joke.

At her soirées she would have guessing games with her guests, some of them quite eminent as art historians, critics and aesthetes. Which one, Sir Harry, is the original? What d'you reckon Sir Charles? Perhaps the Right Honourable Know-it-all in the Cabinet would care to give an opinion of this Cézanne—or that one? This Dali, or that? This Pickersgill, or Rosencrest, or whoever she chose to tease them with that day.

So to call this place safe and a refuge, seemed like the understatement of the century.

"Thank you," Angela said. "If all comes good, maybe I can donate to your collection."

"If it comes that good, my dear, I will be very happy for you indeed, but do mind and be careful what you wish for. Do take care."

Angela finished her tea.

Dame Paloma raised her hand and flourished her fingers. The butler, who was ex-Special Branch and built like a Russian shot putter came over with a black Bakelite and brass candlestick phone on a long extension lead.

"I don't suppose you'll want me eavesdropping," the Dame said and got up and, taking the butler's arm, escorted him to the small caged lift that lived in the wall between the two buildings. It opened either way.

Angela raised the handset to her ear and dialled the number she knew by heart; that of her employer when he stayed overseas, in Prague.

The line crackled hysterically.

No worries there: that suited what Angela had to say.

"Rupert? Rupert? Oh Rupert is that you?"

"Angela? Why are you telephoning on a Wednesday? You must know it's not a good day for me."

Tamarind was closed all day, so he wasn't expecting her, and it was probably his lunchtime. Even better if he had to make a quick decision.

"Oh—I'm so glad I got through to you," Angela said. "See—I'm desperate—"

Here she inserted her best impromptu snivel.

"—I'm in a terrible, terrible situation. I really need, I mean, if you wouldn't mind awfully—"

She could hear the impatience in his breathing. She turned up the pitch of her voice.

"—I—I've had such a horrid, horrid row with my boyfriend and my landlady has thrown me out because of the volume and disturbance and her other residents. She told me not to come back, and I can't go to—," she grabbed a name at random, "Jeffry's place, so I was hoping, maybe just maybe I could crash in the back room of the shop? I mean there's a kettle and a sink and I would be no trouble. I'm sure I can make do. Oh please say that will be okay. Just for a day or two. You see, without—," *dammit*, she closed her eyes tight, "—Jeffry—who said some really horrible things, I'm completely on my own in London."

She could visualise Rupert rubbing his hand up and down the back of his neck, twisting his not quite symmetrical mouth, not used to dealing with a domestic crisis like hers. She allowed him some seconds to think, as if there was a delay on the phone line.

Eventually, Rupert's voice crackled down the line. "I'll not have you stay in the shop. I'll speak to Mary. She can make up a guest room. Stay as long as you like. Tangerine likes you. That's good enough for me. I'll tell Mary."

"Thank you, oh thank you. I can't thank you enough," Angela said. But he had cut her off before she got to the end of her gushing.

She replaced the handset in its holder. She felt a sense of forward motion. She had walked on stage and delivered her first real line. The villain of the piece had delivered his, exactly as he should. It remained for her to choreograph the scene between them, to see how much of the stage she could own, before they spoke again.

She called out to the apparently empty, looking-glass house, "All done. All fixed. Thank you."

Her suitcase sat next to the front door. She entered the security code and let herself out.

It was easy to find a cab. Almost as easy as the phone call.

But as she instructed *Morricone Crescent* to the cabbie, the quiver of a doubt entered her head. Had it been just a little bit too easy?

CHAPTER FOURTEEN

Under a shimmering blue sky, Linda sat at a pavement table outside The Association Bar & Grill, staring at the white tide marks left in her cup by her second cappuccino. She was trying to ignore the square of chocolate cake and whipped cream in front of her, *complements of management, Miss Linda. Today we remember those back home, their past struggle, and all peoples' struggles all round whole world.*

Linda could only accept the gift with a polite grimace. She had arrived with time to spare for her appointment with clairvoyant, fortunist, and all round ear-to-the-ground Abigayle Korah who lived in Stoneycross, the yellow brick low-rise block opposite. Sitting and waiting like this, fighting temptation which the proprietor's family at one time could only have dreamed of, made her feel churlish.

Her fretting over her undying debt to Vic Victor senior now felt like privileged self-indulgence. But she couldn't rationalize such debt away; it was not easily shaken off. Without doubt it was a form of naive, not to say childish, magical thinking. Ten years ago, she had created the duty of debt in her mind, entirely unbeknownst to the elder Vic Victor, and continued to pay interest on the debt to his son, believing the universe would reward her with further kindness, so long as she did not take such kindnesses for granted. The idea hung like a charm over her head and she could not, or dare not, abandon it. She was stuck; she felt bound to MTC and yet the life it afforded her lacked a spark that she craved.

In the middle distance something heavy and hard struck something heavy and metallic, as if a gong had sounded to remind the residents that the local feeding-frenzy of construction, now part of the soundscape of this nook in West London, was not going away.

The Association Bar & Grill nestled on a corner of its own, hemmed in by terraces of sooty London brick dating from the nineteenth century; it was quaintly out of place, like Linda, confined in its own solitude while the world around it changed. Linda couldn't put her finger on why her worries worried her so keenly today. As if she were about to face a great personal loss. As if a pillar of her life were about to be willfully destroyed, to make way for something unwanted and new, like the scattering of yellow-brick post-war blocks, of assorted shapes and sizes, that had been slotted into the gaps created locally by the over-zealous dentistry of Hitler's bombs.

She followed the echos of clanking steel into the distance, wanting the clock somewhere nearby that struck the quarter hour, to strike half past four. She had never been able to work out where it was, but relied on it.

Come on Abigayle! It must be time by now!

Local mothers with creaking prams and passing plumbers with misshapen bags milled about like passengers waiting for a train.

A gold Rolls Royce slid into a metered parking bay in front of Stoneycross.

Then finally, the mystery clock struck the half hour.

Linda turned her attention to Abigayle's telltale kitchen blind on the ground floor, which would roll open as soon as the current client session was over.

Instead, the double doors at the front of Stoneycross burst apart and a tall thin man, grey at the temples, in a black suit and wide red tie stormed out. The chauffeur jumped from the Rolls Royce and dashed around to open the rear door for the man, who Linda now recognised as none other than Harry Dagg, the notoriously vicious gossip columnist.

What would Harry Dagg, friend and enemy of the rich, famous and powerful, be doing in a modest housing trust block like Stoneycross?

As the Rolls Royce slipped away, Abigayle's kitchen blind jerked open.

Linda, connecting the two, got up, crossed the street and let herself into the building.

(Abigayle trusted her established clientele with the main entrance key-code: "Dear heart, I can't be having meself hovering by me front door on tenterhooks, awaiting the ingress of every last seeker of truth now, can I? A life of waiting is a life wasted—no need for second sight, dear heart, for so modest a prognostication.")

The front door of Number One, Stoneycross was thus open, as usual.

Inside, Abigayle's home was a menagerie of lost properties. Each room was themed around a colour: Mediterranean blue, or Popish purple, or Tuscany orange, and each room was adorned with found objects: here a turquoise lamp; there a wall-hanging Persian rug; here a Nativity in golden figurines. Abigayle had even picked up a replica Jacob Epstein sculpture (or was it?). All had been collected from the streets nearby and assembled and juxtaposed with a designer's eye to give the impression of a tented middle-eastern souk. Linda found herself surrounded by objects which had been discarded and left out in the well-to-do streets on the Holland Park side of Notting Hill for whoever deigned to pick them up, rather than have them end up in the dustman's cart.

And when it came to such scavenged artefacts, Abigayle in the kitchen, the far-seeing Abigayle in her rose pink kaftan, all baubles and beads, charms and bracelets, with her bronze skin and rainbow-coloured, beehive hair—she was The Scavenger Queen.

"Dear heart, I just knew you was a-coming!"

"Abby," Linda said, settling into the bench seat at the kitchen table, "I think you must be clairvoyant."

"Ball or brew?" Abigayle said.

Linda's habit was to choose the crystal ball to fathom the depths and consequences of any letter from Ruby Rattler, and to choose tea-leaves to glimpse the shape of her fate when it came to acting on her own initiative. Today her worry was general, non-specific, and yet she shied away from the precision of a grainy silhouette. "Ball," she said.

Abigayle reached for the crystal ball from the kitchen dresser and placed it on the table, making a show of settling it securely on its three legged ebony stand. With a soft amber cloth she smoothed the globe until its surface reflected the ornament-packed kitchen without blemish. After lighting a candle with a steady hand, she let down the blackout blind over the kitchen window, and relaxed into a co-conspirator's posture on her side of the table.

Almost purring, she said, "Hands out, please."

Linda reached across the table, as if to embrace the crystal ball.

Abigayle took the proffered hands and closed her eyes.

Linda, knowing she must play her part, also closed her eyes and watched after-images of the candlelight where it had danced inside the crystal ball. She easily dismissed passing thoughts of Ruby Rattler and MTC but, having seen Dagg outside, she couldn't rid herself of the image of the black suit, red tie, and metallic gold Rolls Royce. They continued to shape the swirls of colour behind her eyelids. Dagg, Linda thought, had been sitting here, where I sit now, and this thought somehow lessened Abigayle's authority, draining her of power, and Linda was unable to enter the usual sensation-free trance.

"It is time," Abigayle said, releasing Linda's hands.

"Your aura is in a state of grand flux. You have important decisions to make and it will be difficult to see what is to come. But never you mind, we will work hard to see through the difficulty."

Abigayle placed the tips of her fingers on the crystal ball and squinted sideways at it.

Shortly, she said, "You are searching for something. You are trying to provoke a change, but you don't want to take responsibility for it. I can't quite make it out..."

She continued to move her lips as if searching for words but saying nothing, until:

"Ohhh, ohhh—what's this I see...?"

Then, frowning: "I see a man. Pacing up and down. His hands flat over his ears. But it's all very quiet. To and fro, he goes, to and fro. Hands clamped to ears."

Abigayle squinted harder at the globe, leaning into it, as if following the man into a distant corner. Once more she was mouthing unspoken words...

Outside, a skateboard rumbled by.

A child called out.

A car door banged.

Eventually, the mystery clock chimed the three quarter hour.

The fortunist looked up and withdrew her fingers from the sides of the glass ball.

"Yes, dear heart," she said wisely. "You are trying to change something. Something in your subconscious demands change, but your conscious does not want responsibility for it. That's all I see today. I can only speak as I find, so, you tell me, what does that resonate with?"

There was no man in Linda's life. Not for a while now. As to pacing up and down and covering his ears—MTC had been kicked out of that noisy ground floor office in Hoxton Square, but that was for not keeping up with the rent. Besides, that was in the past and done with. Surely?

Sensing a dead end, Linda wanted to change the subject to something more productive—to Abigayle's gossip. She wanted to return to the hunt for a story for Vic Victor. She was about to broach that subject when she decided against it. No, not today. She didn't want to appear to be pushy and nosey, having seen Harry Dagg leave the building, which is how it might look.

So, after due contemplation, she reluctantly agreed that she was worried about change, but not sure where it was coming from. "I guess I'll find out the hard way," she said and, feeling disappointed, she placed a brown envelope containing eight five pound notes on the table.

Abigayle slid the envelope into a drawer and released the blackout blind.

When Linda crossed the road outside Stoneycross, the manager of The Association Bar & Grill came out to meet her. He was holding a black cake box with a thin silver ribbon tied around it, secured in a bow.

"In your hurry to talk with your psychic friend,"

he said, "you forget your gift."

"Oh, thank you!" Linda took it with both hands but felt the heat of a blush rising from under her collar. "One day," she said, "I'm sure I'll forget to eat!"

Feeling shamed, she continued in the direction of Holland Park where, after her Abigayle sessions, she would habitually settle her mind as she walked to the Commonwealth Institute to catch a bus home. This time, although the image of a man with his hands clamped over his ears was new and intriguing, it had no immediate meaning for her. Besides, she had a wider worry:

She had seen Harry Dagg leave the building. Was it possible that Abby was a mouthpiece for Dagg? Had Linda, in so many important decisions, been played?

So many times she had used Abigayle's talent to gauge Ruby Rattler's ideas. How stupid had she been?

She pushed open the gate to the park and almost tripped over a football that a toddler had kicked without skill off the grass.

Absent-mindedly, she picked it up and rolled it back. She kept returning to how she was too attached to her debt to Vic Victor senior, all because he had negotiated the bullet-proof contract for her band, *Rap Banter*, before "Go Go Go? Say Ya Mean Wo Wo Wo!" became a global hit. That one decent act, and its supreme legal competence, gave her everything she had today. But it also robbed her of confidence in her own decision-making. Life outside the protected family of MTC was harsher than she knew how to deal with. She knew all this to be true, but knowing it made facing it no easier.

Who was she kidding, anyway? Reliant on the visions of Abigayle, and on the secret letters from Ruby Rattler. She kept placing her future in the judgment of others. How could she know they knew any better than her? She had never met Ruby Rattler, why didn't that worry her? Why was she so reluctant to discover exactly who was behind such an obvious stage name. What was she frightened of?

She left the park and sat down at the bus stop, resting the flimsy cake box on her knee. Yes, she must meet Ruby Rattler; before she accepted further advice, she would seek out the woman herself.

An odd scent distracted her. She lifted the cake box to her nose, and sniffed. The smell coming off it was sour and oily, almost fishy; it could not possibly be chocolate cake.

She prised the lid open, and discovered her favourite sardine salad.

CHAPTER FIFTEEN

It was raining. Moe shivered. *The English summer.* Or did his new life on a narrow boat make him susceptible? Maybe he was just feeling his age...

A gust of wind blasted horizontally along the street, driving rain into the huddled shoppers under the flyover, reversing their umbrellas in the gloom.

Moe grabbed the handle of the locked door to Fabu, steadying himself as he leaned into the wind. Maybe someone had done that before but missed; the restaurant window was cracked.

It was a week since the disappointment of the no-show at Rat Soup. Now he hoped the waitress at Fabu who'd met his informant might provide a description. She might not, but he had to ask. He had no other leads.

You'll be lucky, he'd been told when he returned to speak to her after his wasted journey to Rat Soup. *Next shift, next Saturday, try then.*

Fabu should have opened forty minutes ago.

He stamped his feet. It made no difference. He was cold. The air was damp.

The menu in the window said *Open Daily 11 a.m.*

*   *   *

The waitress whose badge tagged her as Penny, unlocked the door at three minutes to twelve.

Moe pursued her to the counter, pressing his question.

"Pot-belly and silver hair," she said. "Straggly it was. Also, like, he was short, shorter than you, now do you mind, I got people to serve, I got a living to make, okay?"

The dripping wet crowd from under the flyover were pushing and shoving to get into Fabu, and Moe was forced to elbow his way to freedom and stumble, eventually, into the middle of the road.

Stall holders in the street market were hunkered down, squeezing heat out of plastic cups that belonged to Thermos flasks. Moe envied them the heat in their palms. His raincoat was thin and had seen better days. He pulled it tight. He would walk the length of Portobello Road, that's what he'd do. If he saw a short, pot-bellied, silver haired man he would say hello. Then back to the boat. Back to square one. The Harry Dagg story was a dead end. Perhaps someone at the Notting Hill nick would remember Moe from the old days and have a more promising story to tell. He'd just keep trying. Go back to knocking on doors. It was all he knew. All he could think of in the cold and wet.

He felt a tap on his shoulder.

The Malaysian chef from Fabu held up a crumpled piece of paper. "Your fellah," he said, "that fellah you're after, he left this, for 'the man who he look for crime to write about.'"

Moe took the note, shading it from the rain with his free hand. "Thank you."

A phone number was handwritten alongside the words 'BETWEEN 17:00 & 18:00 ASK FOR TACO.'

Well that, Moe thought, is something.

Now his mind was spinning through options for getting a new phonecard. He wondered if maybe he could pull a hotel foyer scam to make a free phone call, but he hadn't seen a neatly pressed suit in weeks. "That's great," he said, less joyous than he ought to be. "You got a phone in there?"

"Only the office—" Perhaps the chef read Moe's disappointment. Or his desperation. "Look mate," the chef said, "yeah, look, come back later and, yeah, use that phone. We're open till eleven, and, you know," he pointed at the crack in the restaurant window which ran floor to ceiling and was patched up with black duck tape, "we could do with some real detective work around here. Do us all a favour."

Moe would have tipped his hat in polite, respectful thanks, except the hat was still at Rat Soup, as a surety for the five pounds he owed.

"I not meet you. No way," a breathy male voice replied quickly at the other end of the phone line.

"But you suggested it."

"It dangerous, like I say. I see last time. He on to you. We only speaks on phone. That all I need."

"Who—who is on to me?"

"I only tell you if you leave me out. You give me your word you leave me out?—I deny anyway. I not even know you."

"Sure, sure," Moe said, "I'll leave you out of this. But I need a name—and an address. *Please.*"

"I give you my wrong name anyway," Taco said.

"Sure. I assumed you took precautions." Moe did not doubt for a second that this man's real name was Taco. "But you can tell me the name of the man in Morricone Crescent."

"May-bee, he call his-self May-bee. Spell it funny though. British spelling. But he the man you want."

"The man I want?"

"You look for crime? He the man of a thousand crimes. He need to be caught."

"Mister Maybe," Moe repeated, hardly believing how gullible he'd been. "And is there a Missus Maybe, a Master Maybe, a Miss Maybe, a baby Maybe?—May be?"

"I know what you think," Taco said. "It silly name. You think I take piss. But no. He take piss. Rupert May-bee, he take piss. Out of British he take piss. You look into him. You find out."

Moe said, "And the address? You have an address for me—in Morricone Crescent?"

"Eighteen," Taco said. "Big house. Very rich man. Nasty. But you, you British, you send him home. We deal with him back home. We know how. We give him justice which system here she can't. You weak and flabby when it come to justice. You, big pussy."

116

"Have you been to the police?"

"I say no more. You investigator now."

The phone line went dead.

Moe thanked the chef profusely, promising to be back every Saturday for a meal once the book was published.

Saturday night and a name and an address. It was hardly Harry Dagg. But very close.

Moe headed towards Morricone Crescent. Worth sniffing around. He even thought he knew which house it was. Maybe there would be someone at home. Maybe not.

Shit. *May-bee?* What the hell kind of name was that?

CHAPTER SIXTEEN

The large bay window on the first floor of Ogden House offered Sandy a view across Bayswater Road over the shrubs, trees and casually neat grasslands of Kensington Gardens. The reception room in which he stood was huge, large enough to fit a full cast rehearsal of anything he'd ever appeared in. It was also neglected. The glass beads of the two chandeliers bathed the room in dirty yellow light, matching the evening sun in strength and colour. The ceiling roses were cracked and grey and the panelled walls, long since concealed behind cheap wallpaper, made the room feel like an old stage set, long overdue the hammer and saw of dismantle and disposal after an extended run.

Sandy watched as a Sky TV van pulled up on the kerb opposite. The paparazzi with their obscenely long lenses milled about like giant insects with giant proboscises, all eyes directed towards Kensington Palace ready to swarm in a frenzy of competitive probing at the first hint of regal activity. It was a fair bet that every one of them was fixated on the cash prize of the front page scoop, hoping to snap that image, the money shot, the image to drive the gossip.

Who would be famous? And yet wasn't that what Sandy, in his own small way, was so desperate for?

No, not to be famous like this. No, he didn't want

this. Not famous for just being. He wanted to be the best he could be at what he did. Of necessity, that involved an audience who shared his passion. An audience that was large enough to support his art. But not this. No.

A police car drew up behind the Sky van.

Two officers got out, but instead of asking the van to move on, they crossed the road to Ogden House, and disappeared beneath Sandy's feet.

A few moments later, Linda, who had brought Sandy along to help negotiate renewal of the rental of the flat as a rehearsal space, called from the door at the back, "Sandy! Here a minute."

The two police officers were standing on the landing. Their faces were stern and lifeless in the dim light.

"Alexander Amadeus?" The first one said, pulling out a notepad. He was the taller of the two.

Sandy confirmed his name, and gave his date of birth.

"Just routine," the second one said in a high-pitched nasal drawl. "Your office said to find you here. Nothing to worry about."

The first one said, "It's about your friend, Stanley—*Stan*—Potter."

"Not exactly a friend," Sandy said. "I went to see him. Once."

"Really?" The second officer said.

"Yes."

"Perhaps you could tell me when and where?" The officer with the notepad said.

Sandy explained that he had the job of finding a real life crime story from the newspapers on which to base a musical. He'd been following up a newspaper report of what had all the hallmarks of a local tragedy. "At the time, it seemed like a genuine human interest story," he said. "The plight of a wheelchair-bound man."

"Plight? Odd word that, sir. Plight?"

"Well, I didn't know he'd passed away."

"So you didn't meet Stanley Potter outside number 16 Morricone Crescent at 11:30 a.m. on the morning of Monday 28th July?"

"Oh, yes," Sandy said. "I bumped into him—well, to be honest he was waiting for me."

"So you met him twice," the second officer said, nasally. "Not once, as you just claimed."

"Well, I mean..."

"Who were you visiting at 16 Morricone Crescent?" The officer with the notepad asked.

"Carlos Nix."

"About what?"

"He had his car stolen. And the car was used... Well, you know, the accident." Sandy felt the blood draining from his face. All the guilt returned over the deceptions he'd perpetrated to get into the two flats.

Having the police confront him, confused him. Which confession did they want? Perhaps both. What could he say? He heard a rasp in the tall man's breathing, smelled peppermint and cigarettes on his breath.

In the dim light, the wide landing closed in on

Sandy like the hated pipe room of the church organ. He felt unsteady. He needed to put his hand on the door frame for support, but couldn't. And there was the habitual childhood guilt feeding his fears, the loss of his father, and the new organist, for whom he could do no right, and whenever accused of the least misdemeanour he would always be guilty, whether he had done the thing or not. In the end you anticipated your own guilt, almost confessing in advance, as the least painful, the only way out...

He found himself stuck in a kind of robotic naughty-step stupor.

The officer with the notepad said, "What do you recall of your conversation with Stanley Potter outside 16 Morricone Crescent. Sir?"

Without energy, Sandy said, "The man was angry. That was all. Blamed Carlos for the accident."

"What did you say?"

"I don't remember. The man seemed, well, to be perpetually angry. I didn't like being around him."

The nasal voice broke in: "You don't remember your own words?"

"No. I mean, I dunno. I just wanted to get away."

"You were seen walking away from the property together." The officer with the notepad said. "Evidently, quite chummy then."

"Can't we get to whatever this is about and get it over with? I mean, can't you just tell me which one I upset so much he called the police?"

"Carlos Nix is pretty upset I imagine," the nasal-voiced officer said, "about being dead. Three days ago. Burned to death. Not a nice way to go."

Linda listened with mounting horror as the two policemen constructed the trap around Sandy. But how could she intervene? She had only the newspaper view of the story he was working on. He'd given away little at the meetings. As though he'd barely made any progress at all. If anything his story was the least promising of any they were looking into; it was so weak in fact, she'd not even bothered consulting Abigayle. *Dammit!* Linda had dropped her guard for a second and trouble arrived in a flash. But it was no good blaming the past. She had to do something now.

Sandy's eyes flicked left and right, from one policeman to the other: a trapped animal facing two foes.

Linda felt the threat personally. Her family was under attack. But she was out of her depth. "He needs a lawyer," she said.

"Please, madam," the taller of the two men said, "if you want to avoid being charged with obstructing our inquiries, you best serve your colleague here by staying out of this."

Stay out of this! Linda was incensed. She could only stare at the man costumed in ill-fitting blue. *How bloody rude!* She had a terrible urge to slap him.

Never in her life had she been in trouble with the police. The closest she had been to a policeman had been when a police line had kept the fans of *Rap Banter* from the band at the Hammersmith Odeon.

She needed to get to the phone to ring Aintree, Bach & Coultishaw, who were MTC's lawyers. But if she went for the phone, at the back between the kitchen and the bedroom, would Sandy be here when she'd finished? She astonished herself by blurting out:

"You can't do this. He has rights you know. It's a free country and he's done nothing wrong!"

"Your name, madam?"

Reluctantly, but somehow pleased to have entered the fray, feeling somehow she was upping the stakes, she gave her name.

"And your date of birth, madam?"

Now she felt judged.

She said the date, then added quickly, "So how'd he die, this Carlos *whoever*? In what fire?"

She grabbed Sandy's hands, which were trembling, raised them and thrust them towards the taller policeman's face.

"You can't really believe this boy—this musician—this artist—could possibly have anything to do with destruction? Look at these. Soft and supple. These are musician's hands, not some arsonist!"

The policeman exchanged a grim look.

"It wasn't arson, madam," the taller policeman said. "It was murder."

CHAPTER SEVENTEEN

Moe Stone assembled major stories on coloured filing cards which he kept in an ancient ceiling-high cabinet rescued from a cinema that had once stored reels of 16 mm film.

The thick wad of variously coloured cards that made up any story reminded him that every story had depth. Each spanned a period of time: had a history, and a future, and spanned people. A story was a three-dimensional chunk of life, even if you experienced it as a sequence of events and typed it up serially in words for your editor to end up in the black and white of newsprint.

Each stack of cards that made up a story was kept in its own shoe box on one of the shelves in the cabinet. He had requisitioned an old box for the story that centred on this May-bee character (pink), and his relation to Dagg (red) and their relation to Taco, the informant (yellow). Question was, should Moe include Morricone Crescent itself as a character? Was there something about it as a place that made a difference? He flexed a green index card against his upper lip and inhaled its stationery office smell...

Outside on the tow path, a couple went by, arguing. A dog scampered behind them, yapping as if snapping at their heels. He was too close to Sainsbury's, opposite

Willesden Cemetery; this section of the canal counted as busy in his terms. It was lunchtime on a Friday and people were winding down, or gearing up, for the weekend. He suspected the yappy little dog would be hoarse by Monday. He was reminded that his spare bottle of gas was running low—so low he couldn't tell how much was left. He hadn't had a shower for three days, expecting the hot water to die on him the second he splodged shampoo—or the washing-up liquid that served as shampoo—in his hair.

No Sainsbury's for him in any case.

He slipped the green card, unmarked, in at the rear of the fledgling wad in the shoe box. For any story, there had to be one pivotal moment during the course of his investigation when the story swung into action; when the story became a thing, took on a life of its own; found momentum. He was not there yet.

That morning he had walked past 18 Morricone Crescent, the May-bee house, and seen the police next door. The front window of the upper ground floor flat at 16 had been blown out. The outside wall was blackened and smoke-damaged. All any of the officers would tell him was that there'd been a fire. Who'd have guessed? He reckoned there'd been a fatality; his instincts screamed *story!* Dagg at 14. May-bee at 18. Taco crying foul at exactly the same time. There was simply too much going on in three adjacent houses for these events to be unconnected. That must be his assumption anyway: find the connection.

He wondered if he might contact the fire service

posing as an inept insurance clerk, wanting details of the fire. He could claim the insurer needed figures urgently for the end of their accounting period, and his boss was on his back, and he had numbers to make up... But he'd need the reliability of a land line to pull that one off.

Outside, a canal boat chugged slowly by, creating a gentle wake that hardly nudged his boat—except that it did, and he realised that it was not the canal boat passing that produced the nudge, but someone had stepped on board.

The slight change in kilter told him the intruder had stepped onto the stern, where the engine was, and where his toolbox provided the only improvised weapons he had: a hammer and spanners. Well, those and an aerosol klaxon, which he kept by the middle hatch. He crept aft, reaching for the klaxon on the way, and then, seeing a shadow move in the rear section that housed his engine, he filled his lungs:

"I'm armed and this is my home. I'm prepared to get ugly—just so you know!"

"No need! No need!" The voice was breathy and familiar, but he couldn't quite place it.

"I'm warning you!"

Silver-haired and pot-bellied, a short man—shorter even than Moe—squeezed through the door from the engine room. It could only be Taco.

"What are you doing here?" Moe said.

"My lunch break."

"How do you even know...?"

126

"I follow you," Taco said. "Last Saturday. I saw you get note and you went to house. I follow you home."

Moe was at a loss that such a cheap detective trick had been used on him while he was trying so very hard, himself, to play detective. "Oh fine!" Moe said. "So what d'you want?"

"It my lunch break, but I skip it. You have any food?"

"Could be." Moe was torn between telling him to sling his hook and begging him for information.

"You find sandwich, I tell you how things change."

Moe relented, allowed the klaxon to drop to his side, turned and made his way back to the galley. He pushed the not inconsiderable clutter out of the way as he went, to make a wide enough path for the man not to knock anything over.

In the galley he bent to open the fridge and extracted a loaf of sliced white bread.

"Not good to keep bread in the fridge," Taco said, slipping into one side of the dinette, which was piled high with shoe boxes.

"If you don't want any, you're welcome not to." Moe said, feeling pangs of hunger himself.

"No peanut butter?"

"No, I do not have peanut butter." Moe fetched out a semi-frozen tub of margarine and a dish bearing a cracked block of cheddar. He elbowed the shoe boxes to one side, to make space for the food. "Lunch," he said.

Taco peeled a slice off the loaf and chiselled bits off the cheese. He didn't bother with the margarine.

"And?" Moe said.

"Your street been very busy," Taco said. "It been very busy indeed. I think you notice, when you visit."

"Sure," Moe said, "the fire."

"More busy. Much more. For starting, mister Maybee, he have himself live-in woman. Nice for him but more difficult if you want to break in, have a look-see inside."

"A wife?"

"No, she young woman. Pretty thing. Dark skin, like from Greece, or you know, but not as white like him."

"Fine," Moe said, counting the slices of bread. "You said, 'busy'. What about the other houses?"

Taco took his time chewing a mouthful. He made a hand gesture for a drink.

Moe filled a glass of water.

"Other problem with you breaking in to have a look-see is someone is watching the house. At least I think it that house. Could be 16 or 18. But someone watching. They quite good, I think, but I see better." He waved his finger in front of his eyes. "I have tip-top viewing place."

"How do you know he's watching?" Moe felt tempted to add *and not rubber-necking like you*, but was aware he might equally be accused of that.

"He also dark skin, to look at. Mediterranean too. Maybe angry father of woman. That all I can say."

"And that's your news? Two unidentified strang-ers?"

"Oh no, mister crime writer. That not my news. That just gossip column stuff. That teaser. No, no. Real news, real crime is murder."

"Murder?"

"Oh yes. Beautiful. Wait to hear detail. This, sort of death that should come May-bee way. I tell you— nothing else in fridge? I not see eggs?"

"They need cooking."

Taco pointed at a bottle wedged onto a shelf at one side of the oval kitchen porthole. "Gherkins go nice with cheese."

Moe reached for the gherkins.

"Number sixteen," Taco started. "Lover-boy of married woman upstairs, he burn to death. Very nasty. I hear all detail—I work close enough to hear, see. Me, no-one notice me. So I hear. He murder real nasty, see. Some guy—and they catch him, he put up no fight—but some guy he tie lover-boy to chair. And under chair he put bucket of gas—petrol—you know. Good big bucket, half to full. And, so the policemen say, a gas cooker igniter, it dangle over bucket, and it wired to the door bell. Lover-boy he wait. Woman, she call. Ouch, you think. Ouch, I think."

Taco paused to refill his mouth.

After much chewing and another glass of water, he said, "But bigger ouch than that. They reckon he had headphones on, playing something over and over for hours while he waited for lover-lady to show up. She find door locked and ring bell. You imagine? Same music over and over. Even Abba get you down in the end. Play too much. Although lover-boy taste in music is hardly worry now."

"Has there been an arrest? Like the husband for instance?"

"Oh no. Man he confess. He make no trouble. He called Potter. He work in gas station and good with electrics. *Woosh!* Imagine. *Woosh!* He blame lover-boy for car crash kill his son. See I am good snitch. Next time you give me better than bread and shitty cheese. Keep a pizza in your freezer for next time. For me. For when we come to real meat and potatoes. For when we nail May-bee."

Moe added links to his mental map to connect these people. A married couple, a cuckolded husband, a car crash, and revenge by someone, a father, who was beyond caring. The tentacles of cause and effect spread wider, but still didn't feel like the tipping point he wanted, or needed, for his story. He had nothing on Dagg. Not yet. But all this trouble on Dagg's doorstep, was there really no connection, nothing to implicate him? Moe could still smell a story and if there was something to find, dammit he'd find it.

"Now," Taco said, "you need to pay me for this. Cash, like in movies. It worth money to you. You write book and make money. You can put some my way. Now I know where you live. We meet regular."

CHAPTER EIGHTEEN

Linda was not happy bringing Sandy with her simply to present him to Joanne Cambridge, MTC's chief sponsor.

Fine, so Vic wanted Sandy to perform his party piece to keep Joanne sweet. "Good PR, Linda my love. We can't afford to lose her, not now." But Linda thought Ms Cambridge, being an especially astute entrepreneur, would want tangible results. In the absence of box-office takings from an enthralled public, well, a gripping score, or convincing script might be nice. Any lesser gesture was a risk, and a star without a part was an actor out of work. Asking for trouble. A risk not worth taking, to Linda's way of thinking.

As she sat with Sandy in the arena-size lobby at Temple Wharf, home of *TranSilicon*, the heavy rain outside shook the large copper-tinted windows in a series of deafening blasts. Passers-by flexed their umbrellas into the wind while the two sets of revolving doors kicked this way, and that, in the gusts.

Sandy had come wearing his interview yellow, albeit hidden under a macintosh and with a trilby that Linda thought looked completely out of place (thankfully now resting on his knee). One of the receptionists had offered them coffee, which they had both declined. The digital clock on the wall gave the time as 12:22 p.m. Eight minutes to go. "A minute of her time is worth five hundred times a minute of yours," Vic had said. "So don't waste it. Knock her out, then leave."

The lift doors at the back of reception juddered open and an elaborately dressed woman marched out. She was clearly of a type that did not belong in any City office which took itself seriously. As she clacked her way on precarious heels to the main desk, Linda couldn't fathom how any woman could look at herself in the mirror and think it was okay to wear a pink polyester top patterned with large blue diamonds, a white stole, and red and brown horizontal-striped leggings. The woman's abundant flesh squeezed out, sleazily, in the most unflattering bulges, and none of the colours anywhere near matched her frizzy dyed-orange hair. The woman was a clown—if not someone to be sorry for. Certainly she did not work for *TranSilicon* or, surely, even hoped to work for *TranSilicon*. But the woman, now at reception, was looking Linda's way. And the pretty young receptionist was nodding and pointing.

12:24 p.m.

The pink-topped woman launched herself towards where Linda and Sandy were sitting.

A wave of irritation stiffened Linda's back. She could do without frivolous distractions. Facing Joanne Cambridge demanded focus.

As soon as the woman was in word-throwing distance, in an accent which was neither properly British nor properly North American, she demanded: "Which of you is Sandy Amadeus?"

"That's me," Sandy said, clutching his hat as if about to get up.

"I wanted to see your face, that's all," the woman said.

"I'm sorry?"

"Not as sorry as you're going to be."

Linda leaned forward. She was not in the mood for some basket-case off the street. Her nerves were jangled enough. "Who do you think you are?"

"Me?" the woman said. "I'm *not* a murderer—that's who I am."

Linda gestured to Sandy to stay seated while she herself got to her feet. She wasn't as tall as the woman in heels, but carried a natural well-proportioned bulk that, she knew, gave her a physical presence. Not only that but a navy blue Thai silk business suit, with matching shoes, completely out-dressed the loud, tasteless creature, and added to Linda's confident physical presence which she now felt to the full. "I think you need to leave," Linda said.

"You deny it then? You deny it?" The woman tee-tered on her heels like a ruffled parrot leaning into the wind. She glared at Sandy, who continued to sit, clutching his hat, clearly baffled.

Linda waved to the receptionists to come over.

"You were there, weren't you?" The woman said.

"Say nothing," Linda said.

Sandy was saying nothing.

"Did you or did you not speak to Stan Potter?"

"Don't answer," Linda said.

"Well, I, err..." Sandy's voice trailed away.

The woman turned on Linda. "I'll have you know I'm a close personal friend of Joanne Cambridge, and she'll be cutting her sponsorship for ETC or whatever you call yourself so long as you employ this *schmuck!* The police may not be pursuing inquiries, but I am."

The male receptionist had arrived and was hovering, uncertainly, making various 'excuse me' noises.

The woman pointed her finger at Sandy and jabbed. "You!" she said. "You! I'll see *you* in court. I'll see *you* behind bars!" And she stormed off, although she struggled when it came to pushing the revolving door against the unpredictable wind.

"You alright?" Linda said, as the noise of the rain washed away the after-screech of the woman's voice.

Sandy's face was white and blank. "Sure," he said, remotely.

"Can I get you a cup of tea or something—biscuits perhaps?" the receptionist said. "Really, I had no idea when she asked if you were here."

"Who is she?" Linda said.

"Madame Jarafat," the man said. "Delores, I think. A friend of Joanna Cambridge. Comes in from time to time. She's a little um, well... She's not usually like that."

12:29 p.m.

The young woman behind reception, who had stayed at the main desk, called across: "Miss Turnbull, you can go up now. You know the way."

134

CHAPTER NINETEEN

The morning after Delores Jarafat's outburst, Sandy felt like he'd auditioned for an old silent movie, landed the lead part, and was now immersed in a grainy absurdist comedy. He was playing *The Removal Man*, who was charged with shifting a piano across London, by hand.

The trouble was: the piano was real; the bit where he pushed and pulled an unwieldy object over uneven paving stones, was real; the journey across London, leastways from Hoxton Square to Shaftesbury Avenue, was real; even the slapstick was real, if unscripted. When he thought of the whole situation in the round like that, it didn't seem so bad. The joke of it would see him through—the only bad news was there was no camera. Any vaguely Chaplinesque or Keaton-like antics would be lost to posterity, and would never appear on his show reel.

Sandy did not begrudge the work, especially since he knew money was tight. Vic Victor had sold the piano that belonged to the theatre some months ago and, having that morning rented the theatre for rehearsals for a sitcom about a boy-band, the old upright from the fourth-floor bedroom podium had to serve as a replacement. It was only Sandy's luck that the cheapest way of getting the piano from bedroom to orchestra pit was not to hire a van, but to lift, heave and push it along the road, with an old patched-up tarpaulin in case it rained, as it had done most of the day before.

Crispin, another Linda foundling, who'd only dropped in to pick up a cheque, had been roped in to help Sandy. Together, they had been kitted out in white painter's overalls as a gesture towards protecting their office clothes, and were edging the piano down the gentle slope to the junction of the Clerkenwell and Farringdon Roads, which Sandy reckoned was the half-way point.

Sandy was shuffling backwards, straining to ease the piano as it jolted from paving stone to paving stone, when his foot sank unexpectedly and a rush of cold water swamped his shoe.

"Wo-ah! Wo-ah!" He pushed the piano back, against gravity and against Crispin. The piano slewed to a halt.

Sandy shrugged off the two wooden wedges joined by a string which were draped over his shoulders. Using his water-sodden foot, he nudged them into place between the pavement and the base of the piano, to stop it rolling.

"You could have told me!" he said, dragging his shoe off and tipping out the water, his sock now clingy and wet.

"You're the one at the sharp end I think you'll find," Crispin said.

The road and the pavement behind Sandy, in the

direction of travel, were flooded. Pedestrians were tip-toeing from one side of the water to the other, trying to time their journeys to avoid the water-ski arcs of brown liquid thrown up by passing cars that were rushing to catch the traffic lights at green.

The piano, on casters, was set to get very wet, and very unplayable, in quick time.

"We're going to have to ask for help," Sandy said, "to carry it to the other side."

"How long have you lived in London?" Crispin said.

It was true. People were already crossing to the other side of the road, even though the pool of water engulfed the pavement on that side too. No one was about to volunteer. Sandy felt every square inch of flesh in the leaden cold of his foot as he visualised the shortest detour—an uphill climb—back and two lefts. And the chance of more puddles. And what then?

He pulled off his sock and started wringing it out. "Back up and go round, then?" he said. But he was already rolling the silent movie in his mind's eye, seeing a succession of longer and longer detours, street after street, delay after delay, getting lost and eventually arriving back where they started, at the setting of the sun...

"No, you're not looking at the problem the right way," Crispin said. "In point of fact, it's a stage manager's dream, can't you see it?"

"Not really," Sandy wondered what craziness this comparative stranger was capable of, and how they would explain some lunatic idea to Vic Victor if, when confronted with the loss of a piano, the great Vic Victor even bothered to take the time to carpet them. "What do you have in mind?" Sandy said, doubtfully. "Dismantle it and carry it across in bits?"

"Why, you got a screwdriver on you?" Crispin said, then laughed. "Nah! We can walk it across, like a fridge."

Sandy knew the technique: you lean the fridge on one edge of its base, pivot it onto a corner, swivel, and drop it back to the ground. Do the same again but with the adjacent corner. Do it enough times and you've moved the fridge. "Yeah," he said, "sure. And the bit about lifting a piano? And getting it wet every time it touches the ground? Might as well push it through."

"Very funny, I'm sure, but do you know how the thing's constructed?"

"In principle," Sandy said.

"Good. There's a metal frame isn't there?"

"Yes."

"And part of the frame crosses the bottom of the piano."

"I suppose."

"So," Crispin said, "we could support the whole piano, without damaging it, by pivoting it directly on the frame, in the middle, like a see-saw."

"Yes, but the pool of water is wider than the piano is long, so we can't exactly reach over to the other side."

"You're not thinking," Crispin said. "Imagine

stepping stones across a stream. We could balance the piano on the first stone, swivel it over the second stone, land it on the second stone, and repeat for the third."

"I see no stones."

"Better still we have two wooden blocks which we can move. Balance on one, move the other forward, balance on that and repeat. We're walking the piano and *bingo-wingo* we're across the water!"

"And we're soaked," Sandy said, thinking this Crispin fellow is going to get his fancy purple trousers doused in London rainwater, painter's overalls or not.

"Sure, but the piano isn't."

Sandy could see the logic, but it still screamed slapstick stupidity to him. What if the piano fell on its side? But he had no ideas for a viable alternative. He shrugged. "We'd better drape the tarpaulin over it," he said. "I mean, for the cars..."

By the time they'd moved the piano half-way across the pool of water, they had a system going, and were in the swing of it.

Passers-by were pausing to watch, creating a queue where the water on the far-side pavement was at its shallowest. They were all too keen to share their opinions.

"Look out, it's sinking!"

"Lost the 'orse?"

"The 'orse is drowned already, init?"

"Which one's Laurel?"

"They's both skinny eight stone nuffings, you twat!"

"Okay, okay, so where's the 'idden camera?"

"You wouldn't catch me with me socks off in that."

"There's a bus coming. Bus coming! Hey lookout, stand back, watch this!"

"Should've brought a hat," Crispin said as the bus drew slowly to a halt, stopped by a red light. "Could've picked up a few bob." He dabbed his brow with the back of his hand. "Apropos of dress codes, my good friend Linda tells me you had a teensy-weensy little contretemps with Madame Jarafat yesterday—I expect it was of her making. Tell me I'm wrong."

"Just what I need reminding of," Sandy said, unable to fathom how life had got so complicated so quickly.

"I know her, you see." Crispin said. "I've come across her a few times, as a matter of fact."

"Yeah? Not easily forgotten."

"No, seriously. She's the one lives next door to Harrietta Dagg. That's the woman isn't it? Morricone Crescent."

"Can we just concentrate," Sandy said, thinking he would sooner never see or hear of the woman again, "on keeping this balancing act going?"

"It's the story you're researching isn't it?"

"Yesss!"

"You're obviously onto something."

"What I'm onto is: pushing my luck and reaping the reward. Whatever I'm on to, I can do without." That, at least, was all too true. He dearly hoped to be moved on, to another story, or for someone else to find a story that was exactly what Vic Victor was after.

"What did the illustrious Miss Cambridge have to say when you went in?"

"She said," Sandy recalled, with at least some satisfaction, "'I sponsor who I damn well like. Making decisions is what I do. Justifying them is not. Vic said you can sing, so sing.'"

"Ahh," Crispin said. "And can you?"

"She seemed happy enough."

"You know the Jarafat woman had a thing going with the guy who died in the fire? Her husband's tenant. My money's on the husband."

Sandy nudged a block into position on the pavement with his bare foot. "Can we talk about something else? They've already arrested someone, as it happens. He's already confessed. Not the husband at all. Someone called Stan Potter, who unfortunately I met."

"You don't know Harrieta Dagg, next door, then?"

"No."

"Father's Sir Harry Dagg, the gossip columnist."

"Fancy."

"She'd have all the goss on Delores, if you wanted. Useful background to the story you're working on."

"Maybe. Maybe not."

"Obviously, dealing with these people is not pleasant. The silver spoon brigade soon tarnish in the clear light of day. But unless you explore all avenues, rule everything else out, you can't be sure you have the full picture, can you? Face it, if you allow the anger of one pretentious cow to stop you doing your job, you could miss the one story that Vic Victor needs. How do you know unless you try? I'd talk to Harrietta if I were you. I'll come with you if you like. I can introduce you. How about it?"

"Haven't you got a story-project of your own?"

"No, I'm not paid for that, being a mere interior designer. You might like to see her place though, what Harrietta—we—have done with it. Quite theatrical in her tastes, she is."

"Really," Sandy said. Although if, this time, he was formally introduced to someone, his research might go better. He supposed. Plus he shouldn't allow himself to be hectored and bullied out of doing a job he agreed to do. He could see that. "Look, tell you what," he said. "You're right. Unless I ask I'll never know. Nice is she, this Harrietta? Bit of a gossip, you say, talkative?"

"Oh, *nice* isn't the word for her, and the word *gossip* is wholly inadequate." Crispin said, adding, "We'll see if she's in, a short detour on our way back to the office."

"Got the hots for her, have you?"

"Not the best choice of word, in the circs."

CHAPTER TWENTY

Moe Stone slipped the health and safety contractor's lanyard over his head. The ID named him as Dan Kovaks and included a mugshot that made him look like Albert Einstein's half-starved brother—he hated the picture but needs must. He patted down the front of the blue-grey uniform that he had 'kept' after once working undercover as a night watchman, and he extracted his bleep box from one of the pockets. The fist-sized orange gadget had a black pencil-like tube sticking out of the top, and three black buttons and a blue bulb on the front. He pressed the middle button. The gadget bleeped and the blue bulb lit up. He was ready.

He climbed the steps at the front of 18 Morricone Crescent, rising above miniature evergreen topiary that said 'money' to him, tugged on the bell-pull and surveyed the street. He was surprised at the clear view into the brief front gardens of the neighbouring properties, and those across the road.

Next door at 16, an unruly yellow berberis had been abandoned and was growing freely. And next door to that, of course, was the Dagg's place, where a patch of diminutive shrubs sat like cabbages in shades of green and brown between the house and the pavement, cut off from the world by a concrete dustbin shelter that looked like a World War II bunker.

He could even see over the top of the builder's hoarding at the front of the house opposite, into a garden of exposed earth, where two men in dirty brown overalls were sitting on a palette of bricks, tucking into sandwiches.

Still, for now Moe would limit himself to the question of Taco and May-bee. Approach Dagg sideways, as it were.

A woman's voice sounded from the other side of the door, "Pleeze?"

Moe flapped open the letter box and spoke through it. "Gas contractor darlin', someone's reported smelling gas. You got a moment? I gotta check."

After a lot of rattled chains and thrown bolts, the door opened wide enough to see a face. The woman was short and hesitant. Moe guessed she was the maid. He waved the multi-purpose badge of the lanyard in her face.

"Gas board," he said. "Subcontractor of same, that's me." He brought the orange bleeper into her line of sight. "Gotta check for gas, see. It can come up through the air gap between the brick walls—you know, cavity walls, and the like. So, see, I got to survey the, ah, air quality in every room which is blessed with a, er, outer wall. This a good time, or should I come back later? Only, I need to do it quick 'cos it's gas see..."

The maid disappeared, leaving the door on the chain.

Shortly, he heard her call out, "Miss Angel-la. You need here at front door."

He didn't catch a reply.

Distantly, on the main road, streets away, a siren came and went, fading in and out on the slow air. Behind Moe, an articulated lorry with loose, flapping covers trundled down the full length of Morricone Crescent, shaking the ground and leaving a trail of diesel fumes.

In front of him, on the far side of the solid door at 18, as he listened through the gap allowed by the chain, he became aware of the soft pad of footsteps on stairs. The gentle clop of soft leather on marble.

A clink, and the door opened wide.

Moe Stone could only stare.

Her skin was the soft golden-brown of autumn leaves. Her eyes were dark and hypnotic and full of laughter. Her hair was a half-combed cloud of wild black cotton—her face and body, in their every aspect, bore the shimmering symmetry of untamed nature...

Slowly, as if emerging from paralysis, Moe recovered some semblance of the process of placing one word after another and finding thought, and meaning.

There were lots of pretty women in the world, he had interviewed enough of them in his time. He'd even married two of them, a long time ago. There were also lots of nearly pretty women who had enough skill— or could pay someone else who had enough skill—to render them what he thought of as very presentable.

Worthy of any magazine cover. He'd seen that, too, many times. He'd met and talked to film stars, people who turned heads in any company, in any room, at any time of day or night. People with star quality—but never before had a woman simply taken his breath away.

...and she was thirty years his junior, to boot. He was too old for this. Yet he could no longer even think why he was here; he had nothing to say.

The woman, who he took to be this 'Angel-la', said in English that bore no trace of any regional or foreign accent, "Can I help you?"

Feeling like his mouth was open and he didn't know how to make it work, he fumbled for his lanyard and offered the badge as his explanation for being. Then he said, weakly: "Er, gas. There's been a smell. Someone said. I've got to, er, check." He managed to raise his bleep box to show it to her. He waggled it in the air like a schoolboy with a cap gun. "Check inside, yeah?"

Angela instructed the maid, to make sure 'Tangerine' was in the play room, and to stay there with her.

Turning back to Moe, she said, "You want to survey the whole house? You want to go over it with a fine toothed comb, see if your instrument can smell anything?"

He wondered fleetingly whether she was mocking him. But why should she? Obviously, she'd heard every word he'd said to the maid and seemed to accept that he was what he said he was. If she doubted him, she'd challenge him, surely, and turn him away?

"I, I must," he said. "As I, er, explained to the, er, maid, gas can come up through the walls, in the cavity, like and it can come out anywhere. So I got to check each room."

"Naturally, I shall accompany you," she said.

"Good," he said, not meaning anything. "You the, er, lady of the house?"

"No."

"May I take your name? I need your name for my, er, worksheet. Prove I've been here, done my job."

"If you don't know who lives in this house, who your customer is, that smacks of very poor service don't you think?"

"I need to check."

"Really? So you're telling me that you are unable to respond to an emergency because you have to fill in a form first? Doesn't sound like much of an emergency to me."

"But the owner, the, er, bill-payer, from our records, he's not here?"

"Mister," she glance at his lanyard, "*Kovacs.* Would you like to follow me into the drawing room so you can point your detector at the wall and take your readings?"

He followed her into the first room and ran the pencil 'detector' up and down the walls, which were papered with a fancy black and white artsy print. He took special care to check the window frames and the skirting, which were painted white. The room itself was modestly but tastefully furnished. A bit like one of those boutique shops on Westbourne Grove which he all but ignored. It seemed very clean though, and smelled musty and unused.

"Finished?" the woman said. "No gas, huh?"

She ushered him across the hallway into the room on the other side.

"This is the living room," she said.

Moe checked the walls as before. The wallpaper in this room was in a similar style, but purple and black, and the easy chairs looked more comfortable, better padded, possibly even used. He had yet to see a television.

"Still no gas?" She said.

"No," he said. "Seems okay so far."

"You haven't asked me if I've smelled gas."

"I, I assumed you'd say."

"So tell me," she said, "if there were a gas leak, would there not have been a conflagration when they had the fire next door?"

"Oh, no, no," he said. "It's because of the fire next door we are particularly keen to, um, check. In point of fact, I was, er, going over the Dagg's place, and, er, we had a bit of a scare, 'cos the cooker was on, and one of the rings wasn't sitting proper, on its mounting, like, so there was excess of, er, gas. Know the Daggs do you? Struck me as a very friendly family."

"I think you missed a bit," she said, pointing at the bottom of a window frame.

It was almost as if, given the sparkle of her eyes,

she was flirting with him except, at the same time, she behaved as if she knew who he was, and what he was up to, and was taking the greatest possible pleasure mocking him.

As they went from room to room, he could hardly concentrate. He felt his every move scrutinized in infinitesimal detail, and it flustered him. Every time he gathered his thoughts to ask about the owner or about the Daggs, he would turn to look at her, catch her eye, and become so disconcerted that immediately he thought better of any such obvious, naive-sounding, question: *What does the owner do? Are you his daughter? How long you been here? Seen the Dagg's place have you? What about next door...?*

All went un-asked.

Eventually, it seemed to him they had visited most of the house, during the course of which he had succeeded only in imprinting the shape of the ersatz detector on the back of his eye. The sum total of his conversation amounted to the repeated question: 'okay, this is all fine, which room next?' He could have walked past a metre-high strong box with its door open and he wouldn't have looked twice. He had learned nothing about the house, its owner, and least of all anything about the Daggs.

"Just the playroom left?" he said, wondering who this 'Tangerine' would turn out to be.

"Mary!" Angela called into the stairwell. "Can you take Tangerine to the roof? We need to check the playroom."

As they ascended to the top floor, Moe felt time was running out and he managed to gather his wits enough to return to the reason for being here: "Seems like a nice, um, neighbourhood," he said. "You, the people next door, the Daggs, and the rest: you all know each other then? Good to have good neighbours, I always say. 'specially when you got a tragedy like a fire..."

"Are you registered with Neighbourhood Watch?" Angela said, as they entered the playroom.

"Yeah, Neighbourhood Watch," he said, vaguely, noticing a television, which somehow was the only thing that made the house feel inhabited. As he ran his detector up and down the walls, he said, "You have to watch them, though. Who knows who joins Neighbourhood Watch. If anyone can join, know what I'm saying? Villains got to live somewhere too, so they're going to take measures. You subscribe to that kind of thing do you?"

Angela gave no reply. She was flipping through a wad of large sheets of paper with crayon drawings and kiddy slogans on them. Just as he finished checking the last wall, she put the drawings down. "No gas, it seems," she said. "I can't smell any. You can't detect any. I think we're safe, don't you?"

On the way down the stairs he asked about a cellar.

Angela reassured him there were no more rooms to see.

Indeed, he was half-way home, still somewhat phased by the mesmerising effect of her, when he realised he hadn't even asked to see the meter. But that wasn't the worst of it. The worst of it was: he had blown his cover for no gain at all. Whenever in the future, he might sniff around the Dagg's place, he was going to be recognised.

Of all the ways to blow it!

Having fetched Tangerine and Mary from the rooftop garden, Angela returned to her room and to the letter she was writing to her mother, about what life in London was like, and how she felt safe, and how the English looked after you... the usual comfort lies.

The truth was: the visit from the phoney gasman had her rattled. She'd done her best to play the domineering and resentful resident, to restrict what he might see, do, or ask. That had not been difficult. He was not merely unconvincing as a gasman, but he seemed not to know what he was looking for. Yet he must have been after something, and if she was staying here, whatever it was, she remained in the way, placing her at risk.

She found it hard to believe he was a petty thief, 'casing the joint'—he was too amateurish—although he might have been 'casing the joint' for someone else. In which case, he'd seen the window grilles and the lockable shutters, so breaking in would be noisy and messy. Also, importantly, he'd seen nothing of any value. When Rupert was away the only things on display were the kind of tat he offered for sale in the shop. Ultimately though, she sensed this gasman's visit was not about simple theft.

She had to ask herself, was it about Rupert? She couldn't believe the gasman was an assassin. If he was, it was one hell of an act. Could he be an assassin's apprentice? No, not really. A professional assassin would not take on someone like that, someone who advertised interest in the target. Surely not.

So what had he wanted? She found it inordinately difficult to think beyond the distractingly amateur character he had created. And he had a smell, didn't he? What was it? It reminded her of wood smoke. Who'd smell of wood smoke in the middle of London? Perhaps he barbecued every meal, his breakfast maybe, set fire to his toast... she had to smile. The English! Life appears orderly and normal, but when you peel away the surface it's all one muddle, if not chaos. Maybe they're a nation of Brazilians at heart.

The wood-smoked gasman had tried asking a few questions hadn't he? Which she'd used her superior stage presence to close down. He'd wanted to know about the Jarafats and the Daggs. He said he'd visited the Daggs, but that was a lie—she'd been at the window and saw where he came from. She saw him put his ID around his neck, and test his plastic toy.

In the two weeks she'd been here she'd nodded a couple of times at the woman she took to be Mrs Jarafat, but she didn't know the Daggs at all. Dagg was the famous gossip columnist, she knew that, but she understood that Harrietta, the daughter, lived most of the time on her own. The daughter was apparently something of an interior designer. She might be an interesting character to get to know. More so if she also was largely on her own. The two of them should definitely get together. It would only be neighbourly after all, and Angela might learn something useful about Rupert.

She resolved to knock on the door of 14 and introduce herself. She could use the fire as an excuse.

As to the gasman. He had at least reminded her that there were people after Rupert and she needed to get her money back sooner rather than later. Another thing, she decided, was there was no Mrs Rupert. She had now inspected every room in the house, just as the gasman had inspected every room, and there was no sign at all of any love interest of any kind, now or in the past. No family photos. No holiday snaps. Who Tangerine's mother was, remained a mystery. But Tangerine's mother wasn't here, not in the UK, because there was nothing to keep her from turning up at the front door and seeing Tangerine for herself—and what real mother would not do that?

But the immediate concern for Angela was to gather intelligence. To make sure she knew everything she could about Rupert. Leave nothing to chance. And Harrietta sounded perfect as a source of local information, and might perhaps turn out to be a good friend in a foreign land. Who knew till you said hello?

One thing was sure, before you strike, you must know your enemy, gather all the information that is easily gathered. You do not want to fail for some simple thing overlooked.

CHAPTER TWENTY-ONE

Harrietta Dagg's house was a mess. Almost as much of a mess as she was.

Whatever Crispin had said that persuaded Sandy to travel this far from either Hoxton Square or Shaftesbury Avenue was now a woolly memory. Entering 14 Morricone Crescent felt like everything Sandy had promised he'd never do again. The intrusion was no lesser for Crispin's introduction. In some ways it was worse because the lie that gained them entry seemed to come so easily to Crispin that it invalidated the chumminess that Sandy thought was developing between them. *I left my Kakkashitsu catalogue behind. Lady Antonia Fraser so wants to see it. Sandy, here, is the P.A. for my new client, Vic Victor, no less.* Sandy saw in Crispin someone recklessly self-assured, and oddly volatile, and sensed somehow that even polite enquiry could turn mid-sentence into a bickering match.

As for Harrietta, Sandy was beginning to think that in this part of London anyone with any time on their hands was, as a matter of course, unhinged.

Harrietta was so striking in appearance that Sandy's eyes kept telling him that her black crepe dress had been randomly slashed to reveal the white tissue lining that now spilled from inside. Her face was long, pink and oval with black piggy eyes, no eyebrows to speak of and a beakish mouth with mauve-tinted lips. Her jet black hair was cut in a fringe which was not level and it was braided with short pink ribbon. She was taller than either Sandy or Crispin but somehow wore it with smallness, with a slight stoop, perhaps, but given the asymmetry of what she was wearing it was difficult to tell. Sandy might have felt sorry for her had it not been for her voice, which managed to be both off-hand and cutting and lacked any resonance or depth—at best it made him think of a bad parody of The Queen.

"You can have five minutes," she said. "But don't touch anything. You know how I like it."

The three of them were standing, awkwardly, in the hall by the bottom of the stairs. Sandy could see into all of the downstairs rooms because the doors had been taken off their hinges and were leaning, some upright and some horizontally, against the nearby walls. It looked like the place had been ransacked, and then carefully vacuumed and dusted.

"Seeing as I'm here," Sandy ventured, "I hope you don't mind my asking, but I met Carlos, you see, and don't know how to approach the people upstairs from him, with my condolences."

Harrietta stared at Sandy as if he were Oliver Twist daring to ask for more gruel.

Not knowing what else to do, and since he had started his pitch, he could only, obstinately, plough on: "I got the impression he had been their tenant for a while, but I don't know if they were close. It sort of boils down to I don't know how to approach them, so I thought maybe, in a difficult time, as their neighbour you could, well, you know, advise, so I don't cause offence..."

"It's the servant's day off," Harrietta said. And, all the while staring at Sandy, added: "Crispin, since you insist on coming back, make yourself useful."

Crispin sloped off downstairs to the basement and, Sandy guessed, to the kitchen.

Harrietta led Sandy into the main reception room which was dominated by a round mahogany table, standing, dead centre, on bare wooden boards. Aside from the table, the room was a building site. All around, pin-stripe wallpaper was either half stripped away from the walls, revealing ancient grey plaster, or bright new sample patches had been applied. Assorted lamp fittings in gold and brass and steel jutted out from the walls, and 'test-artwork' reproductions of Rembrandt, Constable, and Mondrian, had, so far as Sandy could tell, been tacked onto the walls where they might end up hanging.

"This," she gestured to the whole room, "is why I got rid of the last one."

"The last one?"

"That man," Harrietta's head quivered, "making the tea. Mister Campy in the tight purple trousers. That man. He had to go. You can see why. *My god!* Can't you just see why!"

It was impossible to know what, specifically, she was referring to. Sandy saw only a multitude of ideas being tried out.

Crispin appeared with a tea tray. "Your, ahem, maid, Harrietta forgot to replenish the biscuits."

"Well you run along and get some," she said, motioning Sandy to sit down on one of the chairs at the round table.

"Am I re-employed?"

"Not in a thousand years."

"My invoices..."

"Bla bla bla money money money—is that all you people think of? I do hope, mister friend-of-Campy-here, that you have not come to tap me for cash. I don't do cash. I have a butler for that and he's permanently off." Her beakish mauve-tinted lips briefly re-shaped into a cat's anus, in disgust.

"No, not at all," Sandy said. "I just wanted to know what your neighbours are like, so I can pay my respects with regard to Carlos."

"Oh them. I shouldn't worry about them. Not an ounce of empathy between them. They're all money money money, for sure. I can tell you that. Tight or what? Tighter than a quack-quack's whatsit. Money. Don't talk to me about money. Look at this mess, Campy's mess. This costs *money*."

"I heard Delores was quite, er, sensitive," Sandy said, embarrassed for Crispin as much as he was keen to hear what Harrietta had to say about the Jarafats. And then he could get the hell out.

"Her? Sensitive? Madam frog from planet Zog? Give me strength. She's a pretentious foreign do-dawith a gap between her legs that should have been sewn up. And a social climber, to boot. Always has an opinion, but the sort of opinion that she would do much better to keep to herself. Tuck it into that flabby chest of hers and give mister Jarafat something to snuffle around for. Dabbles, you know that? She dabbles. Dabbles in arts and culture and committees and all that. Sits on boards, judges other people—by what right? Dabbles dabbles dabbles. Dabbles a bit too much, if you ask me. If you ask me she dabbled a good deal with that Carlos. That twelve-year-old of recent incineration. Wouldn't surprise me if Mister Jarafat did him in and framed the poor dullard who confessed. Runs a photocopy shop, know that? Little copycat man. Tiny little insignificant, irrelevant copycat man. I got designers in; they got designers in. I got my back garden done; they got their back garden done. I have tea on the lawn—not on the maid's day off of course, or the butler, but he's permanently off—probably taken up interior design..."

Sandy listened, concentrating very hard to feign polite interest. He was performing as, in a sense, was she, and yet hers was real and the word *unhinged* kept coming back to him.

"So, if I were to approach them," he said.

"Oh don't do that." Harrietta placed a hand on his knee. "Don't do that, darling." She turned sharply to Crispin who was still standing under a try-before-you-buy Rembrandt. "And you can stop smirking.

You were the worst interior designer I ever had. The only good thing you ever did was sling your horrid cretinous hook, mister Cramptini, and not a moment too soon, but why you had to trouble me at all—Bah! Come here thinking you'll get paid. Pull the other one, you donkey."

"But if..." Sandy said.

"You are a friend of Campy! I can't believe Campy has friends. I don't believe it. Where do they breed you? Jesus whatsit! Look at his works, oh mighty, and despair. And he wants money for this! Crispin, tell the man, you wanted money. Pieces of paper with the Queen's face on, for this," she gestured at the walls, "and this, and this!"

Crispin reddened. "Harrietta changes her mind a lot," he said. "Harrietta's walls are just as she asked. *Put up some samples darling.* So darling put up some samples. *Take down your samples darling.* So darling took down his samples. Well, I had to pay for it. She bankrupted me and my business, and I'm here facing the blame."

Once more Sandy had entered someone else's life and entered a minefield of other people's conflicts. And yet this time it was not his fault. Somehow Crispin had contrived this confrontation as if he had wanted a witness; he had been determined to come here today.

Sandy felt used and decidedly wanted out. "So Carlos and Delores," he said, reaching for the one fact which was in danger of slipping away, "were having an affair?"

"Child molestation, I think you'll find," Harrietta said, evidently unhappy to have her spat with Crispin interrupted. "Look at the age-gap. Get out your calculator."

Sandy stood up. He'd had enough. "Well," he said, "I must thank you for helping me with my dilemma. And thank you for the tea, but I really must go."

"Like that is it? Like that? A bit of hospitality and you buzz off? And take campy van with you? Well buzz off it is. And don't think you'll ever get money out of me, mister Campoo. You won't."

Sandy got to the front door as quickly as he decently could, opened it, shouted "bye" and he dashed down the main steps to street level, followed more slowly by Crispin.

Only when he stepped onto the pavement did Sandy become aware of the commotion next door. A policeman was standing at the top of the steps, under the portico. Two paramedics were trudging up the steps, carrying a folded stretcher.

And there was the beautiful dark-skinned woman he had seen in Bond Street, coming towards them on the pavement. She was as curious as they were about the police and paramedics—or was it her at all? Was his memory playing tricks? It would be too much of a coincidence, of course. It could not be her.

Crispin arrived by Sandy's elbow and tugged.

"Best not hang around," Crispin said. "Don't let's get caught up in this."

CHAPTER TWENTY-TWO

"You had a bit of a thing for Barry," Vic said. He paused to let a dust cart thunder by on Westbourne Grove. "Never understood what went wrong there."

Linda flushed. Why did he have to bring that up? She took a swig of Guinness from the half pint straight glass in front of her.

The air was muggy, the sky grey. She felt the need to eat, but was not hungry. A sense of defeat arrived from nowhere.

All she had wanted was to establish how Vic's quest for backers was going. They were sitting under a tree in the beer garden at the back of the Earl of Lonsdale, waiting for a promising new lyricist to arrive, any minute now, at half past one.

She wasn't going to let him evade her question.

"What about this Stamford Taylor," she said, agitating the bottom of her glass on the table top, knowing Vic had bumped into Stamford Taylor the night before at the Broadbent Gallery. "He interested?"

"He's got the loose change," Vic said wistfully, "no doubt about that. But he's a publisher, an antiques man, a hotelier. He made the right noises but he seemed a bit shy of the stage. Not convinced that the risk of a dead loss is worth the bet against the excitement of getting past the first night." He shrugged. "May come on board. We'll see. He's launching a new newspaper soon, that'll be, well, you know, eating cash... We'll scrape by so long as we're all square with Joanne. You said we were."

"She was clearly irritated," Linda said. "Described the Jarafat woman as a social Klingon—I'm told that's a Star Trek reference."

Vic Victor winced.

Linda checked her wristwatch. It was 1:32 p.m. She decided she'd grab a sandwich on the way back to the office. "You don't believe Sandy is cut out to write lyrics, do you?"

"He's got his story to work on."

"You heard the songs. He's only just started. He deserves his chance."

"He can sweat the words, along with the grease paint, like everyone else," Vic said. "Earn it. We'll see. He needs to demonstrate loyalty. Barry was everything he promised, Michael Crawford and then some, but then, for whatever personal foible, *exit stage left*. Will Mozart go the same way? You guarantee he won't?"

Linda was unsure if the remark was cheap innuendo. She left it hanging unanswered in the dead air between them. She lacked the energy for a fight. In any case, it was probably just as much of a dig at her sources. Regardless of what she now thought of Abigayle's allegiances, the woman had a gift, even if she didn't know it herself. She had been proved right after all. Sure, Ruby Rattler had discovered Barry, but Abigayle had predicted his rise, *and* his fall. But try telling Vic Victor that Linda, with the help of the two women, had somehow tapped into the grain of the universe and could see how events would play out... Well, she'd tried that line before and he was adamant: *Fate, if fated, doesn't need my help. I'll leave it alone, if it leaves me alone—*

Vic rocked his chair back on its feet and batted his remark away: "Bah!—Linda, my love, I apologize. Nothing to do with you. The guy was an alcoholic. All the signs were there, all the time, if only we chose to see them."

But Linda could not so easily escape her guilty feelings. She had chosen to distance herself from Barry. She had wished him, perhaps driven him, away. Simply because Abigayle had predicted that he would bring the company to its knees. Linda couldn't associate herself with that.

Again she was visited by the image of Dagg dashing from Abigayle's... Could Harry Dagg have engineered the whole fiasco? Some terrible, cynical Svengali?

Surely not.

Because there was always Ruby Rattler. And yet who was she, really? Was she a superfan at all? Could she be yet another face of Harry Dagg, laughing at Linda, laughing at the ease with which he manipulated, one by one, every West End Linda in every West End Company, directing from afar every show, every play, every musical, one performance at a time, performance after performance across the capital?

But why? What would motivate such a man?

Limp and gloomy, Linda felt once more the urge to eat. But she was not hungry.

"Musical Theatre Company?" A young Asian woman in a dapper grey business suit stood by the table. She was holding out her hand midway between Linda and Vic.

CHAPTER TWENTY-THREE

An ambulance and a police car had drawn up outside 16 Morricone Crescent and their engines ticked over with a light judder. People had gathered on the pavement, trying to see above the yellow-petalled tangle of berberis in the front garden as if all their favourite soaps had escaped from television in a single, real-life event.

Angela shivered as she came down the steps of 18 to street level. *Had they discovered another victim of the fire?*

She sidled her way through the gathering and climbed the steps up to the front door on the far side at 14. The four quick knocks she delivered using the polished brass door-knocker made an empty, wooden sound. While she waited for someone to respond, two paramedics carried a stretcher with a sheet over it down the steps of 16. The rubber-necking pedestrians gawped and, across the road, two men were walking directly away from the incident, as if trying to avoid the scene.

Hadn't she almost bumped into them as they dashed down the steps where she stood now? From behind, they seemed familiar, one in tight black denim and a trilby, the other wearing magenta trousers. It was not deja vu, it was more than that, but she couldn't quite put her finger on who they were—or where... She didn't know any gay men in London. More's the pity because there were times she could do with a safe chaperone.

The door of Fourteen opened and a white woman appeared in a home made black Cinderella dress with white painted slashes and lots of loose, faux-silk flaps. The woman glowered. "Yes?"

"I live at Eighteen," Angela said, acting the ever-optimistic local friend-and-confidante. "Your new neighbour, you know?" She angled her head to one side as if everyone knew by now. "Thought I should say hello. Us girls on our own during the day and all that."

Angela felt herself being colour-checked, accent-checked, and fashion-checked. She puffed up the front of her Laura Ashley summer print dress, just enough to out-breast her neighbour. It was at that moment she realised where she had seen the man before. It had been the Adonis; she held her breath, chest out, wanting to turn and look again.

"Do come in," the woman said. "Don't mind the shambles. My IDs darling—*interior designers* to you— they just can't keep up with all my creativity. Breeze-block baboons to a man. You can't get a real artiste these days. Not for love nor money. They've all gone to Paris, or Berlin, or Milan. I blame cheap travel. Anyone can go anywhere, that's the problem, but I expect you know."

Angela stepped gingerly over a cascade of toppled

cardboard boxes on the reception room floor. She said, "There's probably a collection service somewhere..."

"The maid's day off," the woman said. "You have family over here—or are *you* the family?"

"The family has interests all over," Angela said remotely. This had to be Harrietta and Angela would get nowhere unless she presented herself as the woman's social equal. She added, "Daddy has a Mondrian. You are planning to hang a Mondrian there?" She tilted her head, expertly, nodding gently at the atrocious reproduction on the wall, which she recognised as having the colours all wrong. "I think it would work—with the right lighting."

"You're a house guest, then, *chez* May-bee?"

"Oh yes, we've known the May-bees for simply ages," Angela said. "Before he got into, you know, what he got into... least said and all that. Very generous man, our Rupert. Like you wouldn't believe."

"Oh, I see," Harrietta said.

"I thought, being a neighbour," Angela said, "you'd know him quite well. Although maybe your world-famous English reserve keeps you politely apart? By the way, the two men at the door just now..."

"Forgive my curiosity," Harrietta said, "But just what part of the world *are* you from?"

"I know what you need," Angela picked up a vase and examined it, pursing her lips and gently shaking her head in wonder. She looked up brightly and said, "You need a swimming pool! Rupert has a swimming pool. Has he never invited you? You must come for a swim! I insist. I invite you myself. You shall be my guest—until you build one yourself, of course. Wouldn't that be nice? We could both hold poolside parties, for all us girls in the neighbourhood, alternate weekly between us—don't you think that would be terrific?"

Harrietta looked appalled. Her mouth went all goldfish.

Angela put the vase down and lightly placed a hand on Harrietta's flimsy dress and made contact with the cold, hard flesh underneath. "We'll share all the goss! Oh what fun we shall have!"

"You know who my father is?" Harrietta said, pulling away. "You know, I am sure, I am the only daughter of Sir Harry Dagg. He has a reputation, I'll have you know."

Stepping back, Angela showed her dismay. "He's not a friend of Rupert's then?"

"You may well be who you say you are but I have an appointment so if you'll excuse me. Do pop in any time, of course. My door is always open."

Angela found herself herded into the hallway and to the front door. The words 'who you say you are' hung in the air and she was immensely irritated that anything in her performance was lacking. But was there a threat there too? Suppose the Daggs were friends with Rupert and compared notes?

She should be more careful. Not get carried away by the part. Yet a clock ticked loudly in her ear, and other Rupert victims, more able and with fewer scruples, might be days, even hours, away.

"Those two men, who were leaving as I arrived, I've seen them before, are they neighbours too?"

Harrietta mumbled two names which Angela caught phonetically and added to her actor's memory as she was almost pushed through the front door.

Outside, the ambulance had driven off and a policeman was talking to a short, fat red-faced man at the top of the steps at 16.

Angela went home with no fresh idea as to what to try next, but disconcerted by her sudden ejection from the house. She wasn't used to rejection like that and again there was that worry word might get back to Rupert, and she'd be found out.

CHAPTER TWENTY-FOUR

The house-numbering scheme of Morricone Crescent dictated that the four storey Victorian mansion opposite numbers 16 and 18 was not 15 or 17 or 19 but 37 although, for now, the number 37 appeared only as a daub of white paint on the green builders' hoarding at the front. Moe paused briefly at the door in the hoarding to explain that he was Taco's accountant, aware, as he stood there, that he was on full display to *Miss Angela* if she happened to glance across the street at the wrong moment.

The house had been stripped back to brick, with timber braces where it used to have windows, and whole areas of floorboards had been removed, revealing old rough-hewn timber joists. Moe tip-toed his way up the stairs, which creaked, and reached the roof with shooting pains in his calf muscles and not a little out of breath. Stepping out into the fresh air, he steadied himself on the balustrade next to where the silver-haired pot-bellied man was repointing one of the chimney stacks.

There was a great view of the street below and of the houses opposite. You could watch all the comings and goings, and even see through the windows of the upper floors opposite, where curtains and shutters remained permanently open. The significance of the vantage point was not lost on the reporter turned detective.

"You think you clever man you find me, huh?" Taco said. "But I see you coming. I could run easy, if really want."

Moe knew this was not true. Not only was the back garden boarded up, leaving the entrance at the front as the only way on or off the premises. But he had sneaked in from this side of the road, hugging the inside of the pavement all the way, which presented a blind spot to anyone not leaning out of the window gaps at the front of the building or straining over the parapet. He had inspected the building from all angles since following Taco here on that day Taco had followed him back to the narrow boat; no-one could accuse Moe of being slow to learn.

"With a sharp eye," Moe said, "you must see a lot from up here."

Taco slapped a slither of mortar into a horizontal gap between two courses of bricks, and with one smooth movement, he sculpted the surface, sliced away the excess and caught it on the flat of his trowel.

"You must have seen Carlos Nix trussed up, with a bucket under his chair," Moe continued. "Perhaps you saw the fire start?"

The slap, scratch and splotch of trowel against brick continued.

"You must have seen who came in and *attended to* Delores Jarafat," Moe said. "By the way, d'you mind telling me: how did she die?"

Taco reached out to the board where he'd mixed the mortar and tapped his trowel a few times to knock off loose material. He slotted, shaped and gathered the remaining slodder, and reloaded the trowel.

"What mystifies me," Moe said, "is why contact me in the first place? A grudge against Rupert Malinbrough, or something else? Maybe you were trying to set me up for something you'd done—or intend to do. Is that it? Or are you the killer—or a killer-in-waiting? Perhaps I should report my suspicions to the police?"

Moe did not for one second believe Taco was a murderer. But a man does things for a reason or for reasons. Moe folded his arm to show he would wait.

"I not see missus Jarafat die," Taco said. "But I know how it done. And I know who do it to her. And it no good telling no-one because this man he doubtless out of country by now. And I stay out of it. He not from here, anyways. I tell you that for free."

"You say that," Moe said. "You do a good line in saying things, but heh—why should I believe anything you say?"

Taco rested his loaded trowel on the edge of the mixing board.

"I tell you I not care a thing about these coming and going. I care that Ulan Mikov—you know who he—I care that justice catch him up. Missus Jarafat, some kind of hitman do her. Make it look like accident—a little. Just enough so husband know it not accident."

Moe scoffed. "A hitman? To kill a housewife? Spare me the daytime TV!"

"I know hitman." Taco responded angrily. "I seen many in my time. You know nothing, you people here. They look normal. Perfect normal." He waved his hand. "They blend in. Only one thing difference, one simple thing, they do the deed, person die, and they gone. But I see how he do it. He kill her with statue. Big marble statue on top floor. That is to say, one time on top floor." He twitched his nose in the direction of the house opposite. "They would have need some crane to lift it there. The Jarafats, you know. They no need crane now. It come down. It fall down. On her. It fall down all the way through two floors. Now they roll it out from the down stairs. After—you know—they wipe off the blood."

Moe studied the lines on Taco's face, hunting for a giveaway tic, expecting any moment that the lines would break into a broad grin and the man would burst out in laughter, clap Moe on the back and say: *Ha! Had you going, no? Tell me I not!*

Instead, Taco said: "You no believe. You Western pussy. Pah! This man, he make booby trap. Professional job. In-out of building quick. Up stairs. Do business quick and efficient. Down stairs. Away. Probably landed on other side Europe before statue hit deck."

"The other side of Europe?"

"Skin colour, see. And I see his efficiency. Nothing

else. He not even Russian. Russian like to make sure victim know there is no way out for them. This true. But, he—he no Russian. I recognise type. I don't like say. I think I no say. He long gone. He nothing to do with Ulan Mikov. I tell you, is all coincidence—except for maybe plenty greedy unprinciple people move into street like this. Think show off wealth, even if liar, cheat and thief—or worse. What is to be proud of if you steal what you get?"

Moe knew better than to take the analysis of a witness at face value. But even an analysis implied some sort of evidence underneath. "And Carlos Nix?"

"Oh him? He spend long time fuck-fuck Jarafat lady. He sick kid if ask me. I wouldn't fuck her even if pay me lot of money. Especially now she dead. But he set on fire by car crash man. I hear police talk also, and I see what I see. Some sound travel, some not so much. But voices in the street, they bounce off buildings. Hear plenty good up here."

"What about Harry Dagg? What about his place?"

Taco frowned. "Oh you mean next door other way? I never seen him. She about a lot, but I never seen him. People always argue with her, shouting outside her house. I think she get them do work but never pay. Is same with mister?"

"And you only tipped me off to get some kind of revenge on Rupert Malinbrough?"

"You see his woman? I think she something else. But true fact in life: all the bastard, they all get the beautiful women. I think about it. I figure, beautiful

174

women they get hassled, so they got bastard on arm, bastard see nuisance men off. What she like? I see you speak with her."

"We spoke."

Taco leaned towards Moe, suddenly earnest. "And you find safe? I see you looking for safe. You find safe, you find all the evidence, *then* you go to police."

"If only it were that simple," Moe said.

"I tell you one more thing," Taco said, "Which make no sense to me. The police, when they find missus Jarafat, like when they find Carlos, they say wearing headphones. Both they wear headphones. Both they made listen to something before they die. That too much like coincidence. But what sense you make of any of it? World is mad place and this place, for sure."

On his way back to the canal, Moe couldn't help thinking that two murders in the same building, days apart, even if committed by total strangers did sound like more than mere coincidence. But what was the connection, unless it was the husband? And what about this headphone story? Did he believe it? If true it connected the two deaths, surely, but strangely. If it was the husband, maybe it was a recording of illicit bedroom action... But the police would likely discover what was on the recordings—especially what the wife heard, since there was no fire to destroy the evidence. If the headphone story was true, it did look like there was a single trigger to both murders, but what? Or who?

As Moe joined the towpath, his thoughts came full circle to Harry Dagg. Harry Dagg had blood on his hands. Moe knew that, and Dagg knew Moe knew. Which was why Moe no longer worked in Fleet Street and was grubbing a living sending in second-hand copy to local rags and specialist magazines; living off someone else's fridge content between irregular publiser payments; begging the likes of Vic Victor for scraps.

Suppose Jarafat had something on Dagg and Dagg thought to dispose of the problem and at the same time discredit Jarafat? Frame Jarafat for murder. But however Moe massaged that story there was one logical hoop he couldn't jump through. Someone with a more than plausible motive had actually confessed to killing Carlos.

Then, was the headphone stuff just plain wrong—something in the English language which Taco had misunderstood? Would that make it any less of a frame by Dagg?

What could Dagg have against Jarafat?

Who was this Jarafat anyway?

He never knew enough, that was Moe's problem. His whole life story. By the time he knew enough, always for him, opportunity had passed him by.

CHAPTER TWENTY-FIVE

The right-hand end of the shop window for *Taylor's Academy of Arts and Science* was filled by a full-size plaster-cast head of Michelangelo's David.

A low blue partition ran behind the head and across the whole of the back of the window display. Mounted on the partition were two dozen large-format black-and-white photographs of celebrity speakers who had delivered lectures at Stamford Taylor's high-minded club. But if the passer-by in the street happened to look closely over the top of the low blue partition, and happened to peer into the gloom beyond, at four o'clock on this particular Friday afternoon, they would catch sight of Sandy Amadeus, standing at a beat-up upright piano, apparently playing to himself.

Sandy, however, was not alone.

Vic Victor was a member of The Academy by virtue of having spoken there once about *Gaius*. And while a perk of membership was to hire the venue oneself, a perk of negotiating with Stamford Taylor as a potential backer was to 'Use the venue any time you like when it's not in use. Be my guest.'

Sandy stood on the cramped speaker's platform in front of the creative team of MTC, all five of them, seated before him now, plus an Asian woman who had arrived after the session had begun.

Before Sandy had the chance to embark on his improvised story, a man appeared whom Vic Victor introduced as Stamford Taylor. Vic went on to explain to Mr Taylor that every week they had a creative session during which they discussed ideas and built up possible storylines. Today they were working on what they hoped would be the next big thing, a worthy successor to *Gaius*.

Stamford Taylor perched on a seat and cheerfully responded that they had an hour and a half before they had to clear the space for today's speaker who would be Dashal Kryst, the outspoken American psychologist and essayist.

With a flourish, Vic Victor turned to the stage and said, "Cue Sandy."

A little flustered, and anxious enough already for being the last to perform, Sandy said, "Mine is a love story."

He straightened himself before the piano and recited his story in bullet points, punctuating each with a few improvised chords to indicate mood. He visualised himself taking his audience, scene by scene, through a silent movie.

"A woman is neglected by her husband—poignancy—takes up with their feisty young lodger—adventure—in a hurry to get home, the lodger kills someone in a hit-and-run—a *Psycho-Jaws* vibe—she lies to the police, saying the car was stolen—funereal—the lover demands marriage using blackmail—turmoil—the wife comes clean to the husband—

weeping—husband reprimands the wife—anger—but he blames himself, and the blackmailer must have an accident!—a grandiose march to war—the wife now laughs at him—raucous turmoil—remembering why she was unfaithful to the silly pompous little man in the first place—and here I imagine silence—losing face and, losing all dignity, he kills her—accompanied by the anarchy of voodoo dance music, which only ever gets louder as—the lodger comes in and kills the husband, whereupon the police burst in and secure the lodger's hands behind his back."

There was the usual round of encouraging applause which everyone received simply for being brave enough to present their story.

Vic Victor said, "Questions anyone?"

There were a few remarks about what might be the best choice of music for each emotional turn.

"Anything you want to say?" Vic Victor asked Sandy.

Sandy shook his head. "I know it's a cliché but I don't know how the real life story ends. I'm sure the car crash is important, but having two murders after the crash seems disproportionate. I'm missing a key to the story that might make it great, and feel right, and be memorable. Somehow balanced. A fair revenge, if that makes sense. One that is justified."

"The story you have just heard," Vic Victor said, addressing the team, "might be fine for the English National Opera, or a Russian touring company, because they have a name and they have resources to make a spectacle out of more or less anything. What we need,"—he appeared to make a point of catching Stamford Taylor's eye—"is to have a story that creates a spectacle simply by being told. A story that if we mimed it on a bare stage it would hoover in the crowds. Do you think Andrew Lloyd-Weber would run this story? No! He would demand magic. He would demand something that captures your heart, your soul, your mind and the music—that would have to be something to transport you, something spellbinding. We're not there yet, but you're all headed in the right direction. It's only a matter of time."

Sandy felt precarious on the small stage and it was a relief when Vic Victor announced that the piano should be returned to a back room and, Stamford, would you like to meet Sandy?

Stamford Taylor must have been in his mid fifties. He wore a casual tweed jacket, beige trousers and his long greying swept-back hair anointed him with favourite uncle status. There was something intensely whimsical about his face, and his voice when he spoke was an amicable baritone.

"So, you're the new Barry Turtle?" he said.

Sandy had come to dislike the comparison even more than being referred to as mister Mozart. The reference rather spoiled the initial impression. "I suppose," he said.

"Got some work to do, then. Think you can do it?"

"Well, thing is, really, as you can see, it's a team effort."

"So it is. And who's this?"

Vic Victor had pulled one of the piano movers from her task. She was short and had rich, close-cropped black hair and an engaging smile. "Roz," Vic Victor said, "Meet Stamford and Sandy. Stamford and Sandy meet our new lyricist—one of the team of course."

But we don't have set roles!

Sandy offered his hand dumbly. What about merit? What about everyone else—are we not all on an equal footing? With an equal chance? What about authenticity? How could you own a story, really own it, and express it, unless you had lived through it—or at least something like it?

Sandy gazed at the newcomer, feeling the ground shift beneath his feet.

"I've got an aria," Roz said buoyantly to the three men. "I'd love to present it at the next creative session. Could I do that? It's part of a story based on Dashal Kryst's new book, *Courting Crime: The Kentucky Mass Murders*, you know, the one that came out last week. Tonight's event. Contemporary and it might be quicker and more cost effective to buy the story, instead of spending time and energy on all this expensive research. May I?"

CHAPTER TWENTY-SIX

Water lapped in pocket-sized waves along the stone edge of The Round Pond in Kensington Gardens. Tangerine, in her Pink Panther costume—resplendent with matching tail—threw breadcrumbs not so much *for* the expectant swans as *at* them. With each elaborate volley her tail rippled with glee, as also did theirs.

However, while Tangerine was intent on preserving the wildlife in full view of the picture-book facade of Kensington Palace, Angela was wondering what to do about Rupert who was due home today, if not already home now.

There is an intrinsic danger that goes hand-in-hand with a career as an actor which, boiled down to its essence, amounts to the danger of humiliation in front of your audience. But Angela had inveigled her way onto a different kind of stage, and while her acting ought to stand her in good stead, the fact that she had created different stakes, and she had no script, no director, nor any fellow actor to monitor her performance to iron out any giveaway tics... well, all of this made her reluctant to leave the water's edge and head back to the place she must now call home.

Four o'clock struck on the Palace clock and they should already be back for Saturday afternoon tea.

"Come on, little one," Angela said.

"Aw, but they're still hungry."

"Here, give your bag to the little boy over there. Go on, he hasn't got anything to throw. You want to help him don't you?"

Tangerine obliged.

And, thankful that the good deed was willingly done, Angela took the Pink Panther by its tiny mittened hand and they walked back to Morricone Crescent, which was a long walk for one so small.

Tea, of course, was late. Mary had gone out for the evening leaving nothing, since she had not been asked to prepare anything, thus Angela's strawberry jam sandwich was *yummee, yummee but not as good as Mary's.*

Angela, however, had other things on her mind. When, on returning from the pond they had first entered the house, Angela had noticed a suitcase in the hall, but no sign of Rupert. Now she left Tangerine with a bunch of crayons and a Princess Diana colouring book and checked every room to see if he was in the house. With no sign of him above ground, she ventured down to the basement to see if he was tinkering with the swimming pool and his new pump or, even, dare she hope, have the safe open.

The lights were off but curiosity drove her down the glass slabs of the spiral staircase. The smell of chlorine was stronger than before, and the echo of her footsteps on each step somehow more pronounced. She paused at the edge of the darkness and called out:

"Mister May-bee! Rupert! Are you down there?"

There was no reply. She took another step and the lights flickered on.

In a trick of those lights, for a few moments after she caught sight of the pool, she thought it was full, and the water remarkably still. But as she followed the twist and turn of the stairs and caught not the least glimmer of reflected light from the surface of the water, the world around her flipped to a new reality, like the princess-into-witch visual illusion: the pool was empty.

"Rupert? Mister May-bee?"

Her voice echoed back from the tiled walls of the empty space and faded to silence.

The silence itself puzzled her, until she realised the rumble and clunk of the air conditioning was missing. That would also explain the chloriney, slightly claustrophobic air.

But why was the pool empty? Had it sprung a leak? Or had Rupert arranged to have it cleaned and not told anyone? Surely in any case, he wouldn't have left his safe unguarded? Why wasn't he here?

The ladder at the side of the pool reached far enough down that if she went to the bottom, she could still get out. She decided to invent an earring that she seemed to have lost and suspected it had rolled into the pool and, surely, it would be easier for her to search for it now than have Rupert 'get a man in' with an industrial strength vacuum cleaner?

Watching her footing, she climbed down the metal

ladder, cringing each time her hard walking shoes pinged against a shiny rung. Then, worried she might leave black polish marks on the tiles at the bottom, she removed her shoes and for good measure her socks.

"Rupert? Mister May-bee? Anyone there?"

Her voice echoed and died, bathroom-like, to a damp nothing.

She reached the hatch at the centre of the pool and sucked in a deep breath of chlorinated air. Her heart pounded harder than any pre-performance nerves and a vein started throbbing in her temple. The tarnished dome of metal looked very heavy. But she would give it a go. If caught in the act, she could always claim she was checking to see if Rupert had been robbed. Thin gruel, but...

She stooped over and tried to turn the small hand-wheel on top. She couldn't budge it either way.

Was that it then? Floored by the first difficulty?

Unless, maybe, the hatch was already unlatched. It was too much to hope, but...

She straddled the metal dome, wrapped her fingers around the cold metal of the hand-wheel and tugged. The hatch came up, perhaps a centimetre on the side opposite the hinge, but she couldn't hold it and it fell back with a clang.

So she re-positioned herself on the outside of the hinge, placed her bare feet sideways against it, wedging them in, and she grabbed the hand-wheel again. This time she used her whole body weight as well as the fully tensed strength of her legs to pivot the hatch around. It rose slowly at first, while she discovered the most effective angle to tug at, until, suddenly, it swung open to its full extent and she fell away on her side, thudding onto the hard wet tiles, and ended up, bruise-shouldered and akimbo, on her back.

The pain, she ignored.

Instead, she shuffled, on hands and knees, to the newly exposed opening in the middle of the pool.

Where the hatched had been sitting, a rectangular box was recessed in the concrete. Its lid was open. It was empty.

With the feeling you get when you arrive at a station just as the last carriage of the train clears the platform, Angela stared into the abyss of an empty box that was hardly big enough to accommodate her best heels.

Someone had been and gone and got here first. *Godammit!* Nothing. No papers, no cash, no keys, nothing. Not a crooked cent—unless, unless—had Rupert cleaned himself out, and moved on? But no, not without Tangerine. And there was the suitcase still sitting in the hall.

She tested the sides and bottom of the box with her fingers. Tapped her knuckles against the metal. The box was solid. She tested the concrete around the walls and the bottom of the hatch opening. Solid too. She might never get the chance again, so she had better make absolutely sure there was nothing here. Absolutely no chance of any secret hiding place that remained secret...

She checked and re-checked and convinced herself, and there was nothing more to do. Remembering the suitcase, and the absence of the maid, and little Tangerine alone upstairs, she had better get back as quickly as she could, and leave no trace of her exploration.

At least when it came to closing the hatch, through the design of the hinge, the metal dome had settled back at an angle of 45 degrees, which would not be so difficult to shift. She pushed hard against its cold metal edge and it slammed down with an almighty bang that must have been heard throughout the house.

"Rupert? Mister May-bee?"

The only answer to the question was the reverberation of her own voice.

Perhaps he'd had an accident? Could that be it? Perhaps he'd banged his head or been electrocuted while tinkering with the new pump...?

She turned to face the underwater observation window.

There was no light behind the glass, and the strongest image was her own reflection. As she approached, thinking she would cup her hands against the glass to see the other side, she became aware of wiry shapes percolating through from within. They were superimposed on her reflection like the line drawings in Tangerine's book. She took them to be no more than oddities of the glass, until she realised that the score or so of twisted black lines was generated from the score or so of black cables hanging in the underground bay.

"Rupert? Mister May-bee?"

As she drew closer, the other side of the glass seemed to get darker. And she had the thought that he was in the house, even now. Could he be here in the basement?—yet the lights had been off. His suitcase stood by the front door. Was he coming, or going? He must have heard the bang. Was he watching her every move, laughing at the clumsy rookie-crook, stifling his chuckles into the back of his hand? Was the whole scenario a trick, or a trap? How stupid she was!

"Rup-ert!"

She reached the window, crooked her hands between her brow and the glass, and squinted.

For a second time she experienced that uncanny un-seeing of a reality constructed by her mind from her expectations.

Beams of light, like moted sunbeams, streamed through the window into the space behind the glass and, indeed, as she correctly recalled, there were cables strung out across the space. They drifted this way and that, as if in a gentle wind.

In slow motion.

And the brain-flip, when it occurred, was just that realisation. That inversion in the order of reality. That she stood on the floor of the empty swimming pool and the maintenance area was fully flooded—flooded to its full height—with water.

Now, understanding the medium she was looking into, she read the shapes differently.

She studied what was before her. Cables were tangled everywhere. There were pipes and ducts and crates and boxes, and chairs and towels and piles of rags. All were bathed in the half light from the window and hovering, half supported by the water, none of them quite still.

Her eyes were drawn to the rags. Was it a pile of towels that had collapsed when the area had flooded? Or was it a large cuddly toy, a giant teddy bear hidden away from Tangerine for Christmas? Or maybe just swimwear, a wet suit, or a spare change of clothes.

Whatever it was, it was snagged in cables. They had attached themselves to it...

Ahh—but no.

The final shape formed by the rags came to her slowly, reluctantly, as if she refused to recognise it, but it was there. It had been there all the time. In plain sight. Once she could see it, she could not unsee it, not let go of that image.

Rupert *maybe* Malinbrough, Ulan Mikov, con-man and thief, sat bundled up, tied to a chair, bound with electric cable, weighted down by a swimming pool pump. Dead. His head held back at the angle of a scream. Mouth open. Drowned.

Angela felt the full weight of the wall of water before her; it might burst the glass any second, engulf her and carry her off choking and flailing, pin her to the tiles at the bottom of the pool, pound the breath from her lungs...

Thoughts arrived in half-mouthed, half-spoken sentences as she stood before the glass, a chill running through her veins: Where was the murderer? Where was Tangerine? They had to get out. Both of them get out. Now.

In a vague realisation that never formed into words, she understood that life had changed. The focal point on Rupert gone. The future open, and empty. The world big and hostile. Someone else had taken what was hers, believing it to be theirs. There was no recovery from that. Getting to Rupert first had been the thing. To make the first claim. Anyone who was not the first—well, you might as well be last.

All she had was what she had now: her health and her wits and a little more wisdom than before.

Bizarrely, as she backed away from the glass, one particular detail struck her: Rupert Malinbrough in death and, she guessed, during the whole course of his dying, was wearing headphones.

"Angela! Angela! I show you my picture, see."

Tangerine was sitting at the top of the spiral stairs, hugging a shiny metal banister with one hand, waving her Diana colouring book with the other.

"Wait there, little-one. Hold on. I'm coming!"

The only thing for it was to get out of the house without a second's delay. But where to go? Quickest and easiest—and must be safest—was Harrietta Dagg.

By some muddle of necessity Angela extricated

herself and Tangerine higgledy piggledy out of the house and got to the front door of Number 14 and rapped on the knocker in one long continuous panic-ridden clatter.

Now she was out of the house, Angela felt herself going into shock. She knew it, and she knew Tangerine had noticed something was wrong. But somehow the little girl had picked up enough to know she was having to be brave and was resolutely wearing her brave face.

After what must have been a full two minutes, with Angela taking deep breaths to stop herself fainting, there was still no answer to her knocking.

Angela flapped the letter box and called through it.

"Harrietta! Please! Are you at home? We have an emergency!"

Angela listened intently.

She could hear voices, or rather, a single voice. Shouting was it? It was distant, muffled and sounded a bit like the radio. Was the radio on? If the radio was on there must be someone in. Perhaps Harrietta was indulging in a nap, lulled to sleep by some sports commentator ranting in monotonal excitement...

Angela banged the brass knocker again. She hammered with her fist on the wooden panelwork of the door. Listened through the letter box. "Harrietta! Please! Energency!"

Tangerine tugged on Angela's skirt. "Can I help? I can shout *really* loud when I want to!"

"No, thank you, sweetheart."

Angela put her ear to the letter box.

The radio voice was droning on, some of the words repeated, and Angela started to hear full sentences, and they too were repeated. The voice was similar in pitch and tone to Harrietta's, and the reason Angela was starting to understand sentences was because the same three of four sentences were being played over and over, on a loop. Now she heard it for what it was, it was definitely a loop. But somewhere a long way from the front door. Somewhere where, if anyone was listening to it, they would not hear Angela and Tangerine, no matter how much noise the two of them made.

This was infuriating! This was madness! *For the love of Jesus and Mary.* All this madness! Why today!

She grabbed Tangerine's arm, more firmly than she ought, and dragged the small human being down the steps, not knowing where she was going, but crossing the road—anything to be away from both houses—vaguely forming a plan to get back to Harrods. Or where was the police station around here? She couldn't think, but there must be one.

Oh hell, what now? What's this idiot playing at? Blocking the pavement, staring at us...

A man with long silver hair, a pot belly, and his arms out barred their way.

CHAPTER TWENTY-SEVEN

Sandy had earned his Pimms.

He settled in the love-seat in the walled garden at the back of the house where he was staying. He had swept up the leaves below the tree at the centre of the paved area, which Jodie thought a wonderful game, and he had carefully uprooted a whole carpet of weeds from the raised flower beds that butted up against the climber-friendly walls.

Weeding was as much of a goodwill gesture toward his hosts as it was a therapeutic distraction from his lingering disappointment over Vic Victor's about-face, at Taylor's Academy, on Friday. And Roz.

His hosts, on the other hand, had proved more generous than he had any right to hope. They were letting him stay without any sign of tiring of his company. He could only think they had once been struggling artists and knew how much it counted to have the least bit of help.

He was still deeply unsettled over Friday though. It wasn't just that he had started to think he had a chance with his story—murder and revenge were high drama, and finding a single cause for both deaths would nail the plot. But Sandy had believed it when Vic Victor had said anyone in the team could try for any role. And now this Roz woman was coming in as a lyricist, saying 'buy the story ready-made'. Worse still, which was a point he had to concede, if the proposed story came from this Dashal Kryst, who was an international name, well, the story came with a ready-made audience. Who with any commercial sense—or in need of money—could turn that down?

It was deeply disheartening. He poured himself another Pimms. Jodie, lying on the stone tiles with her eyes on him, tilted her head, disapproving while at the same time sympathizing. Sensitive to something, anyway. It was not good to drink alone, he knew, but he could hardly afford to go out, and solitude cleared the artistic mind.

He allowed the sounds of the London streets to perform as white noise to his ears and searched vaguely for patterns in the shadows that ran up the backs of the houses in the next street along; what he could really do with was some live music...

An awful cacophony erupted from inside the house. A great hammering on the front door.

Jodie was up and off, barking.

What now?

The stranger at the front door, who had all the features of a full-size second-hand Einstein doll, produced a press card and introduced himself as Moe Stone, freelance. "But—listen up," he said. "Listen sharp. You'll be keen as mustard on this story—the one I'm working on—Sunshine, *I* could save *you* shed-loads of trouble."

Sandy, restraining Jodie by the collar, hesitated a moment too long and the journalist pushed his way in, trailing a musty smell, which seemed to come from his battered blue bomber jacket. The word *homeless* came to Sandy's mind, yet the press card looked real, and he'd seen enough press cards when he'd doubled up as understudy and stage door keeper for a week at The Royal Court Theatre.

"You can't just barge in here." Sandy grabbed the dog lead from the coat rack, clipped it on Jodie's collar and allowed her to drag him along. "You need to go, or I'm calling the police."

Ignoring him, the journalist continued into the oak-lined living room and headed for the empty fireplace. He nosed around the framed photos on the mantelshelf, turned and, hands in his front jeans pockets like a teenager (he was fifty if he was a day), he sniffed the air.

"Yeah, we can help each other out," he said, as Sandy caught up with him.

"You need to go," Sandy said. "This is not my house and I can't just let anyone in."

The journalist switched on a wide tight-lipped smile, shifted sideways around Sandy and Jodie, and made himself comfortable in one of a pair of matching armchairs.

Sandy glared. He wanted to grab the lapels of that disgusting bomber jacket, drag the man through the front door, and deposit him in a heap, on the pavement. But he lacked the strength or nerve or disposition to make it happen, and he feared letting Jodie loose. Instead, realizing his voice was the only weapon he could use, he made good with a lungful of that: "What do you think you're doing?"

"So, the thing is," the journalist said, completely unfazed, "I'm doing a piece on the recent deaths in Morricone Crescent and I believe you know the family. At least, you visited this Carlos fellow. Then next door. You seem to be a bit of a Morricone-phile, if you ask me. What has been going on? I mean, if you can't help me, I would entirely understand, but I have an editor on my back and I have to give him something. Might as well be the truth. But if I have to make something up—you know—Mystery Stranger Had Hots for Dead Totty—that sort of thing, well I have to. See my predicament? My job, my career, my *raison d'etre*, hangs on getting copy out. So, you know, I might as well have the truth as feed the readers my best guess story, based on a little evidence and a lot of inserting lines between the lines. Hear what I'm saying?"

Jodie made a sudden lunge and almost pulled Sandy over.

"You said you'd save me trouble, not threaten to print a load of stuff which isn't true."

"You don't look that green to me," the reporter said. "I don't think you are, either."

Sandy stood paralysed in the trap. The journalist seemed able and willing to make threats with impunity. What drove people to such ball-breaking brass neck effrontery? That was the thing that kept trapping Sandy. He had no defence against it.

And yet, this man wanted something himself.

Something that was within Sandy's power to give or withhold, or only part-tell.

After a moment or two of face-squirming, Sandy said: "Seeing as you put it like that. Maybe I can help. But we need to trade. I've got something you want. Maybe you've got something I want."

"Trade's good by me," the reporter said. "What you got?"

"First, the people we each know. We can trade a few names to start with."

The journalist obviously knew that Sandy had met Carlos Nix and Harrietta Dagg. He might not know that Sandy had encountered Delores. Would it do any harm to confirm that he had? He didn't think so, so he explained briefly how he and Delores had met, and then mentioned the beautiful woman with the rich black hair who kept cropping up, and maybe she fitted in somewhere?

The journalist nodded thoughtfully, as if deciding how much he would tell in return. He said, "I know old man Dagg who owns 14. Know him professionally. Never met the daughter. And there's the girl—the young woman—on the other side at 18, Angela. Pretty thing, but a bit clueless if you ask me—if that's who you mean with the big hair. That's who I know. So you tell me, what transpired between you and Carlos when you met?"

"One thing at a time," Sandy said. "You said you had a story that would save me trouble. Your turn—."

There was loud banging on the front door.

Jodie went berzerk, tugging left and right, aiming at any conceivable route to get to the front door.

Sandy dragged her into the garden, shut her out, and strode with purpose to the front door prepared to be robust, shouting: "Is this what it's like being hounded by the press?"

He opened the door to two police officers.

Almost as a reflex, he turned his back on them and waved them follow him through the house. Sandy pointed at the journalist: "I take it you've come for him!"

"Alexander Amadeus?" The lead officer said.

"Well?"

"And this gentleman?"

"M—M—whatever," Sandy said, "show him your press card." As soon as he said it, it sank in that the police had come for him. He remembered the unfair treatment he'd had before. Suddenly the idea of allying himself with the journalist, and implicitly with a newspaper, regardless which one, suggested itself as the better bet. He said, "We're working on a story together."

The lead officer took their full names and dates of birth and the second officer escorted the journalist into the kitchen to be questioned separately.

"Well, mister Amadeus, please describe your relationship with Harrietta Dagg."

Sandy explained about his visiting Harrietta with Crispin, with Crispin providing the introduction, as part of working on a real crime story for MTC.

"And where does this Crispin Cramptin live?"

"I don't know. You'll have to ask Linda at the office."

"And this friend of yours, this journo, this Moe Stone. Known him long have you?"

"No, just met."

"Not strictly a friend then, if we were being honest, sir."

"Friend was your word," Sandy said.

"If you say so."

"Why the questions?"

"You know a mister Malin-Bruff?"

"No, should I?"

"You tell me sir."

"I've never heard of the man," Sandy said.

The officer tucked his notepad into his uniform.

"It is my sad duty to tell you sir, that a body has been found at 14 Morricone Crescent which we believe to be that of Harrietta Dagg, pending formal identification. I hope you have no plans to go away in the near future seeing as we require you to stay here, and you will inform us if you are about to change your address. Do you understand what I have just said, sir?"

"Oh." Sandy stared at the fabric of chair where the journalist had just been. He recalled the bizarrely dressed Harrietta, who had worn bright pink ribbons in her lopsided black hair. He said, "Of course. Yes. Not going anywhere."

"And my advice to you sir, is to leave the detective

work to the police. Find yourself a nice historic *fictional* murder for you amateur dramatics. You know what they say—leave death to the professionals."

Sandy didn't like to point out that that was a line spoken by Trevor Howard in Carol Reed's The Third Man. The policeman didn't seem the sort who took kindly to being corrected.

"Oh, and we need to talk to this interior designer fellow. If he gets in touch, you'll point him in our direction. Clear enough for you sir?"

Sandy nodded.

Deep in the pit of his stomach, the Pimms churned and gurgled.

What was happening to him? All the wrong people were coming for him. But he'd only been looking into a newspaper report. A report, surely, that had been scrutinised again and again at the time. Yet as soon as he appeared on the scene, he was somehow the catalyst to the most awful crimes.

He closed his eyes. What was that name? The seaside stage name. The woman who had signed the note. He couldn't think straight. All of his straining to recall the name drew a blank.

After the policeman finished his questions, Moe poured himself a drink from the jug of filtered water on the kitchen worktop and went through to the living room where Sandy was sitting in the second armchair.

The truth was, for the first time in his life, two marriages behind him and all, Moe was emotionally dumbfounded. He'd been intellectually confused often enough, as his brief exposure to higher education had revealed. That, and exposure to the logic of every editor he'd ever worked for—*if you thought you knew what your editor wanted, you weren't listening*.

But until this moment he hadn't realised how much he hated, really hated and despised and loathed Harry Dagg. The damage Dagg had done him. The harm personally, as if Dagg had beaten him up in the street, left him for dead and pissed on the cadaver. His career was in tatters, he had lost his home, he lived on a barge for crissakes, his talent—because he knew he could write, he knew he could do his job, he'd been doing it in Fleet Street for twenty plus years—his talent counted for nothing. Because Dagg had dirt on his shoes Dagg's dirt had to be wiped on something. Or somebody.

When he learned Dagg's daughter was dead, he'd thought sad for her. He'd never known the woman, though she had a bit of a reputation as *difficult*. But what did that ever mean? How many people would say that he, reasonable rational kind and considerate Moe Stone, was *impossible*? 'Difficult' meant nothing. No, sad for her. But when the police suggested he was in the frame for doing her in, his heart lifted. His heart lifted! Of course they couldn't pin something like that on him, but if for one second Harry Dagg thought comeuppance was coming his way, and at the hand of Moe Stone. That was quite something else: Moe's heart lifted! That was how much he hated Harry Dagg. It was a revelation. Even uplifting. Sure, he was sorry to hear about the woman. But he didn't know her. Was he being irrational? Was he going mad? No, he didn't think so. It was just his honest feelings about the oppressive bastard. The legacy of bile had found an avenue of escape. Catharsis even.

He sat down in the easy chair he had assumed as his own. "Smoke?" he said, reaching for a packet which he knew contained three cigarettes.

"Not here," the young man said. "Not my house."

"Sooo," Moe said. "Carlos, yes. Delores, yes. Harrietta, yes. Rupert May-bee, spelled all posh, no, you never met him?"

"Rupert maybe spelled all posh? What's that? A crossword clue?"

"Might as well be," Moe said. "But you're in the frame for his murder. That's what they told me just now. *In confidence.* But heh! I've got a job to do. And you've got a life to lead. So what I need is the key factor that explains how Harry Dagg is at the centre of all this local difficulty because mark my words he is the one it all centres on and you don't know him like I do."

The young man looked amply confused, ready to spill. "How could I kill someone," he said, "who I didn't even know and never met? They can't think that. They'd have to produce evidence—of motive and means—I mean it's ridiculous. They didn't even mention him to me. They even accepted when I said I never heard of Mal-rough or whatever they said. That was him, was it?"

"They wouldn't tell you straight," Moe said. "Oh, no. Met procedure—I know, I'm a journalist remember—met procedure is to go round the houses. Nothing straight. Bet they tried to make you out as a liar, didn't they? Standard trick that. See, I know what I'm talking about."

Moe leaned back in the chair, rested his arms on his chest, and interlaced his fingers. "So, you spill the beans to me," he said, trying to present the case very logically, and reasonably, "and my paper will put up the money for your defence. Can't argue with that, can you? Top barrister and you're away. A rule of the justice system see, whoever can afford the most expensive lawyer wins. It's the law of the jungle as everywhere else, just dressed up in fancy words and fancy costumes. Like Shakespeare in three Acts, if you catch my drift."

"You can't know all this," Sandy said, "everything you've been saying, unless you've been spying on the houses, or following me. Like how'd you know I live here? How do I know you haven't killed these people yourself?"

"Young man. My good friend. I just want what's best for you. I mean—I get to show the newspaper industry in a good light. Justice is ours and all that. Harry Dagg is a piece of work—"

"His daughter has just died."

"—but it will take a joint effort to bring him down."

The young man stood up, rather more abruptly than Moe felt comfortable with. "Look, mister Stone, I don't know anything about all this. In fact my main source of information *is* the newspapers. So unless you intend to write in ever-reducing circles about a story someone else has already published, I think you need to go. The dog has been outside long enough, *hear what I'm saying?"*

Wasted afternoon, that, Moe thought as he shuffled out of the house into a garden square opposite Olympia.

Still he'd learned a truth about himself. That his feelings for Dagg had energy, and depth, ran through him like the words in a stick of rock. Sincerity was not something he could often indulge in. But wow! What liberation! Sometimes empty posturing got the better of one. Dry, stale and cynical. On this occasion not. But there remained the problem of what on earth was going on with 14, 16 and 18 Morricone Crescent? He didn't feel much the wiser about that.

CHAPTER TWENTY-EIGHT

"You are most fortunate that today I have been plagued by last-minute cancellations." Abigayle Korah settled in the seat opposite Linda in the kitchen in the souk-themed flat at Stoneycross. "That is Fate for you. Let us roll with it. I sense new energies at work."

Damn right! Linda thought. It was barely three weeks since her last session but things had come to a head. She squeezed her handbag hard against her thigh. She had crammed this morning's letter from Ruby Rattler into the slim compartment she reserved for bank notes.

Nor did it bother Linda, in the least, that she had absented herself for a whole morning from the office. Another morning of Vic's *Roz this* and *Roz that* and *Roz will bla bla bla what the hell ever she wants...* Linda could do with a rest from that. And how come not one of her sources had ever mentioned this *wunderkind* Roz, waiting in the wings?

Not even the worry that Abigayle might be in hock, somehow, to Harry Dagg—or the other way round—was going to stop Linda getting at a few basic facts, today.

But there are ways, and there are ways.

With a great show of diffidence, Linda said, "Worry. That's what it is, worry. I'm worried about the health of a dear friend of mine, and I've been very upset about it, lately, and I can't get in touch with her. But with your help…"

"Ball or brew?" Abigayle said, quietly. "Which do you feel in your heart would be more conducive?"

"Ball," Linda said. She could observe Abigayle more closely over the ball than when performing one Rorschach test after another over endless cups of tea.

Abigayle placed the ball ceremoniously on the table, lit a candle, and pulled down the blackout blind. "Now we are nicely set, let us focus on what concerns you. You may whisper the details so as not to disturb the humors."

Linda put her hands out, palms down, ready for the customary finger massage. "One of my fans from my singing days." She watched Abigayle's face closely in the candlelight. "I really, really want to meet her, to thank her, for always being there for me, in spirit. But I think she's ill. And I want to be there for her. Can you trace the connection between me and her and offer me some clue, even the slightest clue, as to how she is or where I can find her?"

Abigayle's face showed only concern. She took Linda's hands. "What is her name, my dear, and are you in possession of something of hers, a gift perhaps, something tangible…"

Now was the moment. Linda was alert to the least twitch of Abigayle's discomfort: "Her name is Ruby Rattler."

No reaction.

"Ruby. Rattler," Abigayle said. "Ru-*bee* Rat-*laa*." And she started repeating the name to herself, almost as a chant, "Ru-bee Rat-laa, Ru-bee Rat-laa..." She closed her eyes, her lips moving, but no more sound coming from them. Her eyelids trembled ever so slightly, and her hands relaxed away from Linda's.

After a few moments of this tuning process, Abigayle opened her eyes, placed the tips of her fingers on the crystal ball, and tilted her head as if asking it the question.

But a second or so later, she let her hands drop, frowned and looked up. "It crazy, my dear. Crazy indeed. I get no connection to no Ruby Rattler, yet, just as before, I see a man pacing up and down in a prison cell. You sure your Ruby Rattler isn't a man. And in prison? A Rubin, maybe? Or a Robin?"

Linda had convinced herself that either Abigayle or Dagg must be Ruby Rattler. And that they would both know the set up. Now she was puzzled. At least the woman is canny enough to be consistent, she thought. But in truth, the real trouble was Abigayle seemed utterly and totally sincere.

"You're telling me my Ruby Rattler is a convicted criminal?" Linda said. "A man?"

"Well, no," Abigayle said. "That's the remarkable thing. He's not actually imprisoned, as such. He's just pacing up and down inside a prison. I don't think he's a prisoner."

Linda felt the bewilderment that only comes when

one's intentions are completely derailed.

"I'm so sorry," Abigayle said. "Perhaps he's no desire for contact. Not yet."

"Not yet? What does that even mean?"

"I think he expects you to come looking for him, and he's not ready yet. When he is, he will let you know."

"I received this letter." Linda extracted the letter from her handbag and handed it over. The lingering question was: *Had Abigayle seen it before?*

Abigayle read out loud:

"Dear Heart, Linda,

My health is not so good. I will not last forever. My dearest hope is that your Musical Theatre Company will flourish long after I am gone. I know you are in search of a story and yet the only thing I have furnished you with is a cast. That is about to change. The stage was set some time ago. The players allocated roles and scripts to match. By now they will have played their parts as best they can. No doubt with a wobble or two—life's little perturbations will take their toll on any plan in any battle. But my hope is that by now you have your story, whether you know it or not. You or a member of your cast has merely to tie it all together and announce it to the world.

I am so sorry that you never got back on stage yourself. That would have been a treat.

Yours as always,
RR XX"

Abigayle checked the reverse of the sheet of paper, which was blank, and handed it back. "I don't know what to make of that," she said. "It does sound rather final. You fear this is farewell?"

"I thought I was being helped," Linda said. "Now I feel like I'm being played. And I don't even know who the hell is playing me."

"I can only see what I see," Abigayle said. "I can't report what is not there—whatever Fate withholds from me, She withhold."

Linda put her money on the table.

"Thank you for seeing me at short notice."

She left, both relieved and frustrated that Abigayle Korah, whatever else she was, and whoever else she consorted with, was not Ruby Rattler and had no more idea than Linda as to who Ruby Rattler was.

Linda sat at her usual table outside the Association Bar & Grille, nursing a cappuccino, racking her brains for any encounter she, herself, might have had with Ruby Rattler but not known it at the time. How many stand-out fans—those who created their own *Banter* stage costumes, and everything—how many had she ever met? A handful, but to think of one as Ruby Rattler? No. A couple of times in the past she had taken it upon herself to ask Graham Gillead, the fan club secretary, if he knew Ruby Rattler, but he said he had no-one on record who went by that name.

Linda had never seen the records for herself. She

had the vision of a large filing cabinet. Suppose the entry had been misfiled? Suppose Rattler was under Rustler, or even Wrestler? It occurred to Linda that Graham would be worth another visit and, if she volunteered to do the searching, she would go through every entry in his filing system, read the name of every registered fan, especially—as she thought about it—any fan with the initials *RR*.

She abandoned her coffee and almost ran to Holland Park Avenue to get a cab.

"North Sheen, please," she said. "Opposite the cemetery."

Graham Gillead lived in a tiny two bedroom flat in a post war council house that he had been lucky enough to buy. For health reasons, he worked at home. He was always in, and Linda expected no different today.

He was a short, thin man with a gnarled grey face and a 1970's perm, somewhere between a Kevin Keegan and a Roger Daltry, except it was tinted punk green.

"Go Go Go!" he said when he opened the door.

"Say-ya-mean Wo Wo Wo!" Linda replied.

"Come in, come in, come in," he said. "Take the weight off. Tea or coffee or the hard stuff?"

"The hard stuff, of course."

Linda sat down in the sofa-sized living room and waited for the cocoa.

"Tell me you're reforming," he said. "You can't

come here, unannounced, and say it's just a social. You're reforming, or you're after something." He wagged his finger. "How many times do I have to tell you—I don't autograph my mug shots any more. You'll have to see my agent for that!"

"Graham—I am humbled and ashamed. I am banged to rights. But it is beautiful cocoa. You got anything needs signing, or shall I make my pitch?"

Graham picked up a bundle of vinyl, CDs and pop memorabilia piled on top of an old style lidded record player, and handed her a black felt tip.

"Ulterior motive," Linda announced after she finished the last autograph and handed back the felt tip. "Ruby Rattler," she said. "I'm making a determined effort to track her down. I'm after any clues, the merest hint. Any ideas?"

"You know, I was thinking about her just the other day. Isn't that strange? She's been with us a long time. Must know as much about you as I do. You don't think she's me do you? That would be awful—no shameful. Rest assured I wouldn't do that to you. But no. I have no idea who she really is except, well, Ruby Rattler, that's who! Look, she's got to be a performer, or a wannabe, living outside the tent for whatever reason. With a name like that. Probably very sad. But if she gets satisfaction out of interacting with you and the fan club, are we the ones to chastise?"

Linda said, "I need to know who she is. You, Graham, I trust. But I—well-I just need to know who she is. I was thinking, if you show me where you keep the fan club member info, I would go through it myself, one card at a time, and see if something stands out. I mean, like having the same initials. Point me to the filing cabinet and I'll just hunker down and go through the lot."

Graham shook his head. "Get with the twenty-first century. It's computerised now. I'll let you have a disk."

Before he copied the membership list to disk, they sat at his desk and he searched for the most obvious mis-spellings that either of them could think of, and initials and variations, but found nothing.

Graham patted her knee. "You did it all. You were brilliant. You were Blondiesque *Magnificent*. But, I'll put the word out about looking for Ruby, and if I hear the tiniest pippyest little squeak, I'll let you know. But you were brilliant. Brilliant. So next time I hear your knock on my door, I expect to hear you and the guys are reforming. Is that a deal?"

"Deal," Linda said with her fingers crossed. She put the disk in her handbag, next to Ruby's letter.

Ruby Rattler whoever you are, even if I must reform the band and bolt the concert doors to lock the audience in, whatever it takes—this time: I will find you.

CHAPTER TWENTY-NINE

When the clerk in the Ladbroke Grove branch of Barclays Bank confirmed that *Canal Holidays Brochure, Autumn 1997* had paid the contributor's fee of sixty-five pounds into Moe's account, Moe withdrew the whole sum, bought food and drink in the minimart next to the tube station and then a seven-day travelcard.

That afternoon at four-thirty sharp he started tailing Taco when the silver-haired pot-bellied brickie left 37 Morricone Crescent and headed for Ladbroke Grove station. As a loosely linked couple, they took the Metropolitan Line east round to Liverpool Street, changed to the Central Line and headed further east, and disembarked a few stops along at Mile End.

A silver-haired brickie who was not light on his feet was not difficult to follow at a discreet distance, and Moe trailed him as far as a small terraced house in Medway Road.

It was ten minutes past five. So this would be the location of the telephone that Moe had the number for. Did that mean Taco went to bed at six? That did not seem likely. Did he go out? Ultimately there was only one way to find out. The trouble was, Moe would look conspicuous hanging around in a street like this. It had no front gardens, and no loiter-worthy corners.

And it wasn't plausible he might be waiting for a cab. In any case, he didn't feel altogether safe.

On balance he decided to take a gamble. He'd go for a long walk and come back at five to six, and then smoke his last cigarette on a corner, like he'd been turfed out of his own home.

In the event, Moe almost walked into the pot-bellied silver haired brickie at the end of Medway Road at seven minutes to six. Having dropped back to a safe distance, Moe proceeded to tail the man to The Palm Tree, which was a pub by the canal that Moe knew well, set in the middle of Mile End Park.

Moe settled himself on a bench in sight of the pub, not wanting to risk being recognised by the bar staff or regulars, which was bound to happen if he went in.

It was a long wait, but at a half-past ten Taco emerged, swaying, and joined the canal tow path, which he wobbled along—quite dangerously to Moe's way of thinking—as far as Courtney Bridge Road where he left the canal and walked a hundred yards or so to an old warehouse which advertised 'chepe rooms' over a double door which, a little open, shed long slithers of yellow light across the street.

So Medway Road was just some place to eat. Who-ever lived there wouldn't have Taco stay over.

Moe walked up to the warehouse door, found no sign of Taco, but he did see that the doors were 'locked strick 11 pm - no exepshions.'

The 11 was underlined and, as Moe paused outside, it was five minutes to.

The door-stepping journalist in Moe recognised a trap when he saw one, and this trap could easily be set, and sprung, and he was the man to do it.

The next day Moe repeated his surveillance but this time when Taco left the Palm Tree, Moe darted ahead, parallel to the canal, speed-walking to the far side of the next road bridge. He slipped down to the towpath where the only illumination came from the windows at the side of the canal and, exactly as he remembered, the towpath under the bridge was lost in pitch blackness.

There was no one else about, no one was foolish enough to use the towpath at night. Indeed Taco probably thought it a safe bet for getting home a little the worse for wear. Tonight, however, Taco walked straight into Moe.

Moe felt a slight disgust at physical contact belly-to-belly with Taco, but he knew that physical shock was the best thing to get the encounter started, giving him instant advantage and the upper hand.

The strong fingers of two strong hands prodded Moe.

"What this?" Taco said.

"Hello Taco." Moe pushed the man back. In the dark, not knowing where the canal edge was, this was intended to be disturbing. "I need your help."

"I got no money. I spend my money. You search me please. You take all I got. I no problem to you."

"I don't want your money, Taco." Moe said. "I want you to tell me something."

"I scream. And police they come. I scream and they take you prison. No good robbing old men. Police no like such things, I promise."

"You scream?" Moe said. "You scream and I'll throw you in the cold water and disappear into the night. You scream all you like but by the time someone finds you and fishes you out, you will be cold and wet and you will have to spend the night on the streets because that flop-house you stay in will have closed its doors. Oh dear me, we are wasting time. You have less than five minutes to get back as it is. What's it to be Taco? What's it to be?"

"What you want? What you want?"

"I want to know where Angela is. You know pretty Angela, and that little kid, Tangerine. You need to tell me, or else it's a cold wet night on the streets for you— if someone comes to fish you out that is."

"No, you can't do. I can't swim."

"Maybe you'll float."

"I not know where she is. That's the truth. I not know."

"But you watch the house. You watch the house all day, don't you? You cannot help yourself but see them leave. And follow them. I know you, so: where did they go?"

Moe gave Taco another shove backwards, Moe having the advantage that he could see Taco in silhouette against the floodlit pub.

"The police, they come. They go away in police car. I no follow police car. No car. I got no car. Not me."

"That's better," Moe said. "But I think you can do better still."

"Ahh! I know you. I know who you are!" Taco said, recovering his bravado. "Now I know. You Moe Stone who live on canal. Why don't you advertise to know where girl is? Huh? Instead of mugging old men in the middle of the night? Why don't you..."

Moe grabbed Taco and swung him to the canal edge—as best Moe could judge while, at the same time, wedging his own back into the brickwork of the bridge, gaining comfort and all the mechanical advantage which it offered. He said, "She came back though didn't she? Women come back for things, like clothes. She came back and you followed her, somewhere. Don't tell me you didn't. Naive I ain't."

Moe could feel the man trembling.

"Look we do deal," Taco said.

"I'm doing a deal now."

"You pay me, I tell you."

"Do I look rich?" Moe said. "Besides, you got everything you wanted, didn't you? Rough justice for mister Rupert whoever-he-was. You don't have to hang around. This is just a loose end. So, you tell me, where are Angela and Tangerine?"

"I tell you, but you have to pay me. I got nothing.

That man, he ruin me. Look at me. You think I choose this life? You give me something. I know—you give me brass clock on wall in your galley-kitchen. You say I have that, I tell you where you find girl."

Moe considered the clock. He'd had it a long time. It had once hung in the family home, a long time ago. He could not just give it away, except, maybe. "Okay, you can have the clock, but I need one thing more. You saw who went into the house and bumped off mister Rupert, tell me who did that *and* where miss Angela and Tangerine are, and you can have the clock."

"Okay, it deal. You put me down, I tell you all. Only now you help me get back to rooms, be locking doors any time now."

CHAPTER THIRTY

Angela sat opposite Tangerine at a breakfast table laid with a white embroidered tablecloth and with sprigs of small white flowers in a clear vase that had been set down between them.

Dominique, the French factotum to the demanding few, served them egg soldiers on gold-rimmed plates with gold-rimmed egg cups in a room taken directly from the pages of Stately Homes England—if any such magazine existed. It certainly didn't feel like a hotel in Central London, not that Angela knew what a boutique hotel in Central London should look like. Or, for that matter, smell or sound like. Wax polish, a solitudinous quiet, dark-stained paintings, brass and leather riding tackle, rosettes, and a fully antlered stag's head mounted on the wall seemed to fit the bill.

"I 'ope you please to enjoy," Dominique said.

There were only four tables in the small first floor dining room. In the far corner, farthest from the window, a man hunkered down over a full English breakfast, pretending to read *The Times* but looking up too frequently to be serious about the news. He was short, round, red-faced, big-nosed and monkishly bald with a skirt of black hair that trailed over his ears, badly in need of a trim. Angela decided that his face belonged on the front of one of those steam engines in the Reverend Awdry railway books that Tangerine kept pestering her to read.

The man was her neighbour, of course, Luce Jarafat. She'd never met him before and even now he barely acknowledged her existence when she insisted, at every one of those ever-so-English polite opportunities, on saying hello. It seemed he had decided they had nothing in common even when they were holed up together in adjoining rooms, with an armed police officer never more than a few metres away.

The current shift-officer was a woman, built like a gorilla, which was really quite reassuring. The officers came and went in four-hour shifts, giving the impression that Angela and Tangerine, Mary who had already breakfasted (and was reading Stephen King in the library), and their stuffy neighbour were the ones in custody. They'd been thus incarcerated for over a week, escorted once a day on a walk around the park and, with mostly adult movies to watch on the video, and bored with board games, Angela and Tangerine had taken to experimenting with hair styles to match those of models in the numerous glossy magazines— until Angela's hair had started coming out in long threads. So now they spent time thinking up things to do when, eventually, they got out of here.

"We can do an escape," Tangerine said, very seriously as she dipped a strip of toast into runny egg yolk. "That's what Postman Pat would do. If he got trapped in his van. That's what they always do on TV, you know. You were on TV. Daddy said. So you know what to do. I can be your assistant." She dribbled the limp, wet toast into her mouth, leaving a great splodge of yellow on her chin.

Angela stared at the child, reacting to neither manners nor mess. *Oh my God, he knew!*

Tangerine chomped on the mouthful.

Eventually Angela fumbled for a tissue from her handbag and reached over to tidy up Tangerine's mouth and chin.

"When did he say that, sweetheart?"

"He said. Before you came. He said I would get a new mummy but only if I liked you. He said you were famous and in hiding. And it was our secret. Now you will have to be my mummy. After the accident."

"Yes," Angela said, not meaning anything at all. "After the accident."

Rupert—*Ulan Mikov*—knew all along who she was and even *had designs on her body...!* Numb physical disgust spread from the pit of her stomach while any understanding she might have had of recent events fell apart in a jumble; she faced a montage of flashbacks to the shop, the house, and the pool that once seemed like stages on a quest, but now they felt like a trap that had almost completely closed around her.

Her whole world flipped on its head. Her understanding of her situation reversed.

The police, she realised, were no less ambivalent in their role. She had to ask herself: was she a witness or a target? A part of her wanted to scream, another part run, and yet another part cower and hide in deeper, darker ignorance. What previously had been a nuisance, but seemingly well-managed, suddenly felt dangerous. She saw no reason why she should be a target, and yet had association with Ulan Mikov turned her into one? As for this creature, Jarafat, she could easily imagine him in someone's gunsight, he oozed callous indifference and must make enemies as easily as a dog sniffs the bottom of its friends. But anyone coming for him would, necessarily, want to leave no witness standing.

With a new clarity, it was obvious that Taylor's Nook, cutesy private hotel that it was, was no longer at all safe. In fact, she did not deem it beyond the bounds of possibility that the police, as they did in the movies, had housed the four of them together, under the same roof, to draw the assassin into the open, into making a move...

And yet, were there not different culprits for each of the murders? Some already in custody? Not one of them, it seemed, had offered much resistance and even wanted, according to one of the armed officers, to let the whole world know why they done it—although the police (and The Home Secretary, Jack Straw himself, no less) did not allow that sort of bragging to get any media time. However Angela, even when she heard about such deranged individual testament, couldn't help thinking there was some bigger picture that they all, everyone now involved, were missing. Because you simply can't have so many murders in one place by coincidence. You simply can't.

And the child? Was the child at risk? Who could possibly even want to kill a child?

Watching Tangerine mining the last of her egg reminded Angela of the possibility of escape. But where to? And for how long before the police caught the person who had set the murderous turmoil in motion? Angela knew no-one in London, that had been the point of coming here. Well that, and a new career. Even the Adonis, who she'd run into twice (and what were the chances of that?) she only had a name for, no address, although she guessed he was a musician from their first meeting, and that he was probably gay from their second—Harrietta Dagg had managed to mumble his name, but that was as much use to Angela as a silk fan in a tropical storm.

Maybe she should sneak back to Morricone Crescent and hide there? The three of them could survive, as it were, in plain sight. There were three cabinet freezers and they were all practically full. Somewhere along the way Ulan Mikov had picked up the habit of hoarding. And if it was a crime scene, and forensics had done their bit, once the three of them were inside, with an officer outside, would they not be as well protected as they were here? Safer, in fact, for being away from Jarafat and the assassin who would be after him. Understandably after him—Angela felt a little guilty in admitting.

Or was she thinking stupid? A stupid risk-taker? Was she the dumb broad phoning home when she'd been expressly instructed not to? Did she really believe the four of them were sitting ducks, bait for the next-in-line of however many assassins were already lined up?

And there it was: *she had been the dumb broad!* She had gone back hadn't she? *And they let her!*

She was distracted from the idea of escape when Dominique planted a fresh pot of coffee and a big glass of orange juice on the table. Angela was forced to watch in embarrassed silence as the factotum started brushing up the bits of eggshell and crumbs of toast that littered the fancy table cloth.

At 11 o'clock the officer who was their regular fresh air escort knocked on Angela and Tangerine's bedroom door, ready to accompany them on their daily promenade.

He stood over six feet tall in a grey suit that was too small for him and walked with a kind of apologetic stoop, ducking under every door frame whether he needed to or not. He was not obviously armed, although Angela assumed he had something up his sleeve, or tucked in a sock, or holstered under his armpit.

Taylor's Nook was a short walk from Kensington Gardens but the officer, whose name was Kenny, insisted that they use the Marlborough Gate entrance, which was twice as far to walk but avoided the paparazzi and avoided getting caught in any chance photos in the *scrummage of desire for a glimpse of*

Princess Di, as it were, madam.

"I don't like it here," Tangerine said between slurps on a cola bribe as they walked slow circuits of the Italian Gardens. "Can't we go somewhere else? They don't make Mary come here."

Angela knew that somewhere else meant the Round Pond. Tangerine refused to go where there was no water.

"I need a wee."

Angela gave Kenny a look. He replied with a resigned smile. It had become something of a ritual. She took Tangerine by the hand to the Ladies nearby, where Tangerine dashed into a cubicle and locked it noisily.

Angela tidied her hair. Expecting a long wait.

"Hello Angela."

A man in a utility uniform stood behind her, in the mirror, like a hammer over a nail. He was wearing a ridiculous lop-sided blond wig and a dark bushy moustache.

It took Angela several, long, heart-stopping seconds to read the face behind her, and know who he was.

The lookalike Einstein; the phoney gas contractor.

CHAPTER THIRTY-ONE

Linda Turnbull broke her own private rule of ten years' standing and, in a business known for excess and substance abuse, sitting alone at home, she poured herself a second glass of Cabernet Sauvignon.

At least, she reassured herself, five o'clock was long gone.

She positioned a hard chair at a useful, draw-tugging angle in front of a green metal filing cabinet. The cabinet loomed over her and was stuffed with correspondence, filed by date, not by correspondent, for fear of ending up with almost as many name-tagged dividers as pieces of paper. The upshot was that inside this cabinet, if she was prepared to search, she could expect to find everything she'd ever received from Ruby Rattler. Somewhere inside, there must lie the clue that would reveal Ruby Rattler's true identity, would guide Linda to Ruby's doorstep and, Linda hoped, lead her to truths of greater standing than those she gleaned from Abigayle Korah.

It was going to be a long night.

She started with the bottom drawer, dating back to when she was discovered, playing in a pub in Limehouse. She had wangled a gig accompanying herself on the piano every Wednesday night when the place was almost empty. And there it was. She'd completely forgotten. The first fan letter. A hand-written note to her, left behind the bar. Why did she keep it? She supposed she must have been touched by the moment. Her first ever fan. She unfolded the note.

Love it. Love it. I lurve it! The note read. *Love of God tho' darling—get yourself a bigger stage. Aim high. Drive hard. Be persistent. Be resilient. Kiss and make up along the way. You will go far and I know just the band for you. Ring this number and ask for Jerry. Love you to bits, darling, RR XX*

Linda was dumbstruck. Ashamed. She ran her eyes over the note a second time.

How could she have forgotten her first fan letter?

Ruby Rattler had been there from the start.

How could Linda have forgotten that?—She stared at the paper and could only think, of course, she must suppose, that the initials RR meant nothing at the time. Just some A&R type, moving and shaking, stirring the pot, plying trade or whatever.

But, Ruby Rattler had sent Linda to Jerry, good old, dear old Jerry, who had got her the audition with Rap Banter. Jerry who had long since gone the way of everything so soft as flesh.

It was Ruby all the way. How the hell did she miss that?

RR XX.

Did Ruby Rattler work for a record label? That would make sense since, later, after Linda's mugging, and after Linda started working for MTC, Ruby had shone a light on Barry Turtle and most recently Sandy

Amadeus, with others in between, like the beautiful Evie Doherty. Maybe that was it. Maybe Ruby was someone who promoted talent to the right place, whenever she saw a promising artist but was unable to recruit that talent herself. In an industry like this, doing something like that, you most certainly would want to remain anonymous, simply to remain effective.

Linda rifled through the letters, the photos, and the cassettes from wannabes who had recorded themselves singing in their bathrooms. And here was another Ruby Rattler:

Linda, dear Linda. You're in need of a good show biz lawyer. Believe me. I know the company you keep. Can't hurt to try now, can it? Be honest. Judge for yourself. Make what you will of Vic Victor on this number. He's the best. Trust me. RR XX

It was hard to swallow. If, half an hour ago, Linda had asked herself who Ruby Rattler was, she would have said, "Oh, she's a superfan, you know. An insider's insider. Shares the goss. A good nose for people, a great tipster for trends." But this Ruby Rattler, the one she'd forgotten, was so much more.

Ruby had made Linda.

How could she have missed this fact—allowed the details to fade so completely from memory? As she sat there in the Central London flat she owned, on a hard chair, in front of a metal box that clanked and rattled with the secret hopes and aspirational dreams of her fans, outside—outside, there stood the ridiculously expensive mansions of Eaton Square which paraded themselves a dribble and a spit behind Buckingham Palace. The homeland of the absurdly wealthy. And what was Linda doing here? Linda was here only because old Vic Victor senior had drawn up the most amazing, awesome, bullet-proof contract for her and the band, such that they received unheard-of royalties, usually taken by the record companies as a matter of course as they habitually fleeced newcomers on entry to the business.

There was no doubt that she could trace everything she owned to Vic Victor senior. Which she happily acknowledged. Had she not dedicated her post-mugging career to MTC by way of undying gratitude? It was the least she could do. But again she had never made the connection all the way back to Ruby Rattler who in those days had simply signed herself RR.

It was shaming.

Struggling to concentrate, Linda resumed rifling through her correspondence.

Soon enough, and once Rap Banter had started selling out venues, RR became Ruby Rattler and the fan letters took on the more usual feel. There were photos of gigs, taken from the audience. Wishlists of tracks for the next album. Newspaper cuttings Linda might have missed, 'for your personal scrapbook.' Although now, a little creepily, seeing the volume and nature of the correspondence, it started to feel as if Ruby Rattler, previously an informative insider with a jocular music-hall name—well, she was evidently somewhat obsessed with Linda.

Was Ruby in love *with Linda?*

Linda felt a twinge of alarm at the thought of obsession, but also horrified with herself at her wanton neglect of one so very generous. Linda had wandered the world and wilfully left her prime beneficiary behind.

She moved to re-fill her glass. The bottle was empty.

Ruby, Ruby, Ruby—you deserve so much more than ever you got! Yet what could Linda offer an anonymous fan?

She didn't even know where, even vaguely, Ruby lived. London was the best guess, but it was only a guess, for easy access to the gigs. Ruby might live in a suburb or commuter town. Ruby might live in another beating heart of musical activity: Liverpool, Manchester or Coventry. Maybe Ruby perpetually toured the country. A&R Ruby, always on the move, was that her?

What Linda needed, at the very least, was a few postmarked envelopes. But envelopes were thrown out; the filing cabinet was jam packed as it was. It was worth a look though, wasn't it? She might have kept something out of curiosity...

She hadn't seen anything so far, but an envelope might have ratcheted its way to the bottom of a drawer. Was she going to tip the whole of every drawer out?

Yes, if she had to. But first she was going to open another bottle of wine. She convinced herself that a slice of brie from the fridge would limit the damage tomorrow.

*   *   *

Refilling her glass, she remembered she had an envelope in her bag. Hastily checking it she discovered it was postmarked Paddington. Well, if they were all going to be like that, it was not going to be much help. You could live anywhere in the country and get to a mainline station if your priority was anonymity. She resigned herself to up-ending the cabinet, hoping for a slip-up, and, in the end as a reward for her persistence, it was not an envelope, but a picture postcard that provided the answer.

The postcard showed a colour-wash drawing of a boy in the countryside, sitting on a stile playing the fiddle. There was a his dog at his feet, dancing on its hind legs.

It read:

LT my dear, I've been listening to my records for old times' sake. Some are nearly worn through so that in their old age they make you crackle a lot. But I want you to know how much joy you bring. How much joy you have brought. Such wit and humour in the music you make. I only wish you would go back on stage before it's too late. Ruby xx

There was a postmark on the card. Faint and smudged, but there was the date: 15 Jan 1996. And there was the place: Dinnridge Post Office.

With terrible glee, and terrible foreboding, Linda's flesh tingled.

Had she found Ruby Rattler? How terrible was it going to be? It might go either way. Did she have to prepare for the worst? Dinnridge, after all, was an infamous village just outside London. A small village, probably not as many as a thousand people living in the village itself. A visit to the post office, an explanation and a smile, might get Linda to meet any inhabitant of her choosing—in the village itself.

But Dinnridge drew its infamy from the reputation of its hospital. A grim red-brick building, stained black by a century of London smog and pollution; a survivor of Victorian enlightenment and visible from the outskirts of town, with its famous tall tower which, depending on who you talked to, disguised either a water supply tank or the smoke stack above an incinerator.

If Ruby Rattler was not to be found in Dinnridge village. Well. Linda's heart jittered.

CHAPTER THIRTY-TWO

Sandy's brainwave was to ask a policeman or, as it happened, a policewoman.

Tamarind in Bond Street had been closed for days and no-one nearby seemed to know where Angela (as Sandy now knew to call her) had gone.

He did not know what role, if any, she played in the story he was pursuing, who she might know, or what information she might have but, thanks to Moe Stone, he knew she lived at 18 Morricone Crescent. It too had been abandoned and cordoned off and the three houses next to one another were now guarded by a police officer, albeit sitting in a car outside, playing solitaire.

Sandy's brainwave was to ask the policewoman behind the wheel of the car where his 'girlfriend' Angela had gone.

"I'm afraid, sir, we can't give out such information," the officer said. "Can I have your name please?"

Reluctantly, Sandy gave his name, and produced his musician's union card as ID.

"Wait a minute." The officer opened the glove compartment, slid out a clipboard, and glanced down a list. "No, no. I'm wrong," she said. "You should have said. You're on the list. You'll find her a Taylor's Nook, it's a small hotel just off Westbourne Grove. Take your

ID, and don't share her whereabouts with strangers."

How his name appeared on any such list was a mystery, but he was not going to look a gift horse in the mouth. The only problem was, when he arrived at Taylor's Nook, he spotted that dreadful journalist sitting on a bench on the opposite side of the street.

The burgundy front door to Taylor's Nook was set into the wall between the *Shangri La* restaurant and *Rodeo Fashion*. It was easily missed by most passers-by, but not possible to enter without Moe Stone seeing him.

Sandy ducked into the *Café Nero* a few doors along behind the journalist, and decided to wait and see what happened.

After nearly an hour, and three lattes later, a clock nearby struck eleven and a tall shambling man in a tight-fitting grey suit pressed the doorbell for Taylor's Nook, and was let in.

A few minutes later the beautiful Angela and a small girl with Shirley Temple hair came out, accompanied by the man, and they headed south, towards Kensington Gardens.

Moe Stone stood, lobbed a brown hold-all over his shoulder, and followed them, staying about a hundred metres behind and noticeably not rushing when they disappeared out of sight around corners.

Sandy followed Moe, but was less sanguine about the possibility of losing sight of his subject.

Eventually they arrived, by the longest route possible, at the furthest entrance on the north side of Kensington Gardens.

Moe slipped around the back—but not into—the small rectangular building that was the public convenience. Angela, the girl and their minder walked in laborious circles around the fountains of the Italian Gardens. Sandy felt like he was watching a play that had been rehearsed time and again and yet every time the actors missed a critical cue. He sat on a bench with a good view of both public convenience and the fountains, pulled his jacket tight, and waited.

In due course, Angela took the little girl to the Ladies. The minder took the opportunity to go to the Gents. A figure in a badly-fitting boiler suit, wearing a badly-fitting blond wig and trying to hide a moustache with his hand—who was obviously Moe Stone—deposited a *No Entry* sign in front of the Ladies, and darted in.

Sandy was immediately on his feet. The last thing Angela needed was that unscrupulous little man. He ran full pelt for the Ladies, dashed, unthinking, past the *No Entry* sign, and arrived just in time to see Angela and Moe staring at each other in the mirror.

Sandy had not the least clue how to fight, but he could run, and he could barge, so that's what he did. He thought only to land his shoulder in the middle of Moe's back and knock the guy out of the way.

Moe caught Sandy's eye in the mirror and was mid-turn when Sandy made contact, his shoulder into Moe's arm, which twisted round into Moe's chest on impact.

Moe fell over, with Sandy on top.

Somewhere behind or above them, a toilet flushed.

Sandy filled his lungs. "Run!"

Angela grabbed the girl and headed for the door.

Sandy scrambled up and tried to follow, but Moe caught his ankle and Sandy had to kick the flailing hand away. Then he too was through the door and following Angela, who was carrying the girl in her arms. They were all running south-west, not quite into the sun, towards Kensington Palace.

Sandy caught up easily, took the girl from Angela, and the three of them ran on.

Somewhere behind them Moe's voice rang out. "You bastard I'll have you!"

Somewhere, even more distantly, another voice announced: "Stop! Police, stop!"

But a gusting wind and the woosh of fully laden branches drowned anything after that, and by the time the three fugitives switched course due south, and had passed the pre-Raphaelite statue of the horse and rider, Sandy slowed down, breathless, and looked behind. He saw no-one who showed the least interest in their flight.

He could only hope that anyone who even noticed them took it to be a game with the child.

The tiny sunken garden at the back of Tom's Deli on Westbourne Grove had the tight uneven close-to-nature atmosphere of a tree house, with a stepped floor that branched out at odd levels, and in odd shapes, and was fanned by foliage from four smooth thigh-thick trees that snaked up the enclosing brick walls.

Like a tree-house, with tightly packed, precarious little tables and chairs, it was where small children could play out their fantasies while the adults could share intimate confidences, as if entirely alone.

Sandy felt like the child in hiding but was struggling to be the adult, worried that the adult thing to do might get the three of them killed.

"It could be the husband," Angela said, nursing Tangerine on her knee, stroking her arm. "Kill the wife and the lover and bury the crime among some random killings—misdirection."

"You've met him," Sandy said. "Is he capable of bending complete strangers to his will? What sort of man is he?"

"Rude. Nondescript. Businessman. Hoggish somehow," Angela said. "No, you're right. He's not enough of a man to make his mark on the world. Except by accident. You can't murder four people in such a convoluted way by accident."

"Execute, I think," Sandy said. "Each murder had its procedure. Like an electric chair. Question is, is Luce Jarafat next?"

"Or me?" Angela said.

"I don't know. You realise there is someone else. Whoever lived in the basement at sixteen, who it seems has just disappeared."

"You mean the first victim?"

"Or someone who knew it was coming," Sandy said, "and got out. If we knew the why of it, the bottom line *why*, we might know whether we—you Angela, and Tangerine—are safe."

"I could go back to the hotel," Angela said. "I probably should. I'll ask Luce who it was that lived in the basement, and what happened to them."

"I don't like it," Sandy said. "You've only just escaped."

CHAPTER THIRTY-THREE

"One pound fifty," the woman in the green, silver-braided uniform said. "For each fifteen minutes, or part thereof. Cash or account?"

"Cash," Moe said.

"Pay on your way out. Ticket the other side."

Moe pushed against the shiny metal bar of a turnstile which gave way with a grinding clank and, as he came through, the mechanism spewed out a card with a crossword pattern of perforations cut into it. He slipped it into his jacket pocket, counting seconds under his breath, irritated that time was money.

The false-ceilinged, closely partitioned room was barely six metres along each wall. All available space was taken up by bank after bank of card indexes, leaving narrow walkways between them.

The only light came from two low-watt bulbs hanging unprotected from the ceiling, making it uncomfortably difficult for any one of the dozen people crammed into the tight space to read anything at all.

Worse than the poor lighting, the heat hit Moe like an open oven.

He slipped his jacket off, but was already sweating, as was everyone, and the air bore a stifling underarm stench that made him want to gag.

He braced himself. This he must do and must do it against the clock.

However, once he started searching indexes he became wholly immersed in the nightmare. It was a necessity of geometry that if one person stood, or stooped by a card index, flipping through cards, it was impossible for someone else to search an index in the same vertical stack. Granted, you might go in sideways, your face against someone's crotch, but even when he reasoned that a few seconds saved here and there might translate into a cooked meal rather than a cheap sandwich, he could not bring himself to stick his face thigh-high against a complete stranger.

Thus a search that, had the place been empty, might, with all the cross-referencing he would have to do, take perhaps twenty minutes, promised now to take more than an hour and a half.

An hour and a half in hell.

He tugged off his tie and unbuttoned his shirt. The sheer revulsion he felt to the job, to the task, to the chore only made him more angry and frustrated. And slower.

More often than not he had to start searching a whole drawer again, simply because his anger robbed him of concentration.

Eventually he got his first useful hit:

Luce Jarafat had been the shareholder and executive director of Mogletti Ltd. Jarafat had bought into the company and been appointed a director in 1980, seventeen years ago. Jarafat was named director or shareholder on a dozen or more companies, but all the other mentions came and went, like someone signing in and out of a job. Mogletti was different. Benedetto Mogletti had been the sole owner of Mogletti and the transfer to Jarafat was of all the stock.

The company was dead, overlooked, and it had been struck off by default. It looked like an oversight. An error. Whoever managed the company accounts had not closed it down properly or sold it on neatly, suggesting someone, probably Jarafat himself, had forgotten about its existence.

When he caught errors like that, Moe knew there would be a trail to follow. He repeated the searches he had made for Jarafat but this time for Mogletti. Mogletti had declared residency in the UK in 1979, and had briefly been associated with Cyprus Holdings, one of whose held companies, after more time, bad air, and ripe crotches, turned out to be Matterhorn.

Matterhorn! That name rang a bell. My God—why did that name ring a bell?

Moe tried to think back twenty years. What was he doing twenty years ago? He'd been on a local newspaper, surely. Or had he? Well, sometimes not. As part of his journey to Fleet Street he had written investigative pieces on this or that, whatever took his interest at the time—to keep it authentic—and he would send his fully investigated pieces to a Fleet Street editor, with a begging letter, CV, and photostats of his best clippings.

Matterhorn had been one of those. He must still have the files. He never threw anything away. This had to be the key. Luce Jarafat *was* Benedetto Mogletti who was escaping his own history, whatever Matterhorn was.

Moe slammed the tray of index cards into their rack, and pushed his way out—anyone obstructing him was robbing him of time, and money. And money was food.

As it was, he ran to one hour thirty seven minutes.

He scraped out all his loose change to escape the room. What the hell did he paid taxes for when he had to pay for so-called public information like this? He could have had a half-decent curry for the amount this hell hole had stolen from him.

There it was in black and white, the whole story in his own professional (looking back, perhaps rather pretentious), reporter's prose.

The Solino Bridge Collapse. 1979. 28 people dead. 30 or more severely injured. The blame was laid at the door of Matterhorn, the company that managed the architectural drawings. Their chief engineer, one Benedetto Mogletti, had simply copied and mixed and matched missing drawings with the wrong versions. The enquiry found he had even changed version numbers by hand to make them match the requests of contractors.

In his article, Moe had listed the dead and the

injured and given a summary of their professions. And here was one name, oh yes, a name that might have the wherewithal to reach out from the past and tap Luce Jarafat on his cowardly runaway shoulder. Lionel Zitzer, defence attaché at the Israeli Embassy! He lost his wife and child. Their car had balanced on the edge of the bridge for four hours while the rescue services tried to get to them. After four hours, it rained and the car went over the edge. Yes, that would really piss me off too, Moe thought.

Benedetto Mogletti disappeared before the official report came out. Suppose Lionel Zitser had just located him, just now, and set about dismembering the Mogletti family, an eye for an eye. That made Luce Jarafat the ultimate target. It made the crime smart and its execution sophisticated, but equally, Luce Jarafat was not going to die. He would merely have to endure what Lionel Zitser endured.

Moe thought, maybe he could scrape enough together for a curry after all. Maybe he should, to pat himself on the back, because even without any mention of Dagg, he'd just struck gold.

CHAPTER THIRTY-FOUR

Angela explained to the protection officer that they'd got lost in the park when they ran away from the journalist who had ambushed them, and oh dear, we seem to have caused a lot of concern but we're okay really...

Were she truthful to herself—as any actress ought—a few lost-and-frightened-girl-in-London tears helped. But in life you have a duty to use what you've got and, as with any skill: *use it or lose it.*

Luce Jarafat sat like a blob on a Regency chaise long in the common room at Taylor's Nook, both feet resting on a foot-chair. He was sipping complementary pink gin and staring blankly at the large screen television which was showing the top 100 all-time great wrestling bouts.

"Hello," Angela said as Tangerine set up a game of Monopoly on a fancy low table which was covered in Arabic lettering.

Silence.

"I'm sorry about your wife."

Silence.

"Tangerine and I—we have lost someone too. It might be good for us to talk. Share memories. Accept what—"

"We have nothing on this subject in common." Luce said, pumping out words in short, abrupt syllables, not taking his eyes from the television. "Is nothing to talk about it. Now, I concentrate. Please."

"We may be in danger."

"You yes, you may be in danger," Luce said. "Me? I no in danger. I never done nothing wrong. Who want harm me?"

"But everyone who lived in your house, and mine and next door," Angela said, "Even your tenant in the basement, you know what I'm saying, even your neighbour in the basement has disappeared."

"Him! Oh, we best off without like of him."

"Why so?"

"You leave me be please. Else I call armed officer, have you removed." He turned his head away from the television and shouted, "Garçon!"

Dominique came swiftly into the room.

"I like something eat with my drink and I have another of these while you about it."

"You were saying about the man in the basement," Angela said.

"He neurotic artist type, fancy himself singer but hate music. How stupid that?" Luce's head lolled around to face Angela. "You not think? Man he say singer, but he hate all music. Pah!"

Luce's glass-holding hand shook and he splashed pink gin on the chaise long.

"He was a singer?"

Luce's face reddened like he was about to explode.

"The man, he never stop complaining about the noise, huh? Never, never, never. *You* turn music down he say. *You* put carpet down he say. He then build stupid installation in hees flat. Like he some kind sculptor. Fill up whole room. He nutter I tell you. We best off when he leave and take stupid installation and all trappings with him. Good bye. Now, you leave me watch sport."

Angela said, very softly. "But a name? Did he have a name?"

"Barry," Luce spat out the word. "He Barry. Barry Cubical or Cuticle or Musical or Murtle or Tittle, Tattle, Truttle maybe even Turtle, he slow and he thick. He no good to no one. Now we end. I done knowing—some useless wannabe, he, who never come to nothing. They come to London all bright eye and flop, like that, they flop. Real life hit them. Pah! Trottle maybe. I think. Barimore Trottle, wow! What a name! Stupid name. Actor made up name. All stupido. Now you leave me alone!"

Dominique arrived with a tray of assorted cheeses and wafer biscuits, and twelve pink gins in identical cut glass glasses in two neat little rows.

Angela decided she rather liked Dominique and after all this was over, Angela would come back here and they'd go out on the town together.

All this time Tangerine had been watching Luce Jarafat with her finger resting in her mouth, as if she didn't quite understand this intriguing lesson in life.

"Shall we leave the angry man to himself?" Angela said in baby tones.

In slow deliberate movements, Tangerine nodded her head.

"Not going out are we, madam?" the armed officer said as Angela passed him at the common room door.

"Upstairs."

It wasn't too much of a lie. She and Tangerine had to go upstairs to get to the fire door that opened directly into the ladies changing rooms of *Rodeo Fashion*, next door.

CHAPTER THIRTY-FIVE

Sandy reckoned that if you were going to hide in plain sight, you should do it properly, so he and Angela set up office outside Bow Street Magistrates Court, where there were five phone boxes.

They took it in turns, one to pretend to be the queue outside their chosen box, playing *I Spy* with Tangerine, while the other made a call. Then they swapped roles.

"No, not me," Sandy said into the telephone. "I'm from Clemens, Atlee and Bacon and we are trying to trace a recent occupant of 16 Morricone Crescent. His name is Barry Turtle and he has been favourably mentioned in a will. Did your company by any chance provide a removal service in respect of said person or address, transporting any furniture or contents or fixtures or fittings from that address, so we can contact the gentleman in question?"

A pause. Always a pause. And a reply in the negative.

"Well thank you for checking."

Angela reported similar responses.

Soon they had reached the end of their list.

"Nice idea," Angela said.

"Someone had to do the removal. That installation of his, it was pretty huge."

"Maybe there are specials," she said. "I've seen vans marked computer removals and office removals. We at least should try them."

Sandy slipped back into the phone box and started thumbing through the yellow pages, pencil and paper in hand.

"Yes," Angela said, "that's me. And we represent the estate of the deceased. Douglas—yes with O-U—Fairburn and Bromley. Yes, yes. But not the man who inherits. That's Barry Turtle and he's still alive, or so we believe. It's just that... Okay not Turtle and not under Barry... Okay, okay and can you try Morricone Crescent, on the off-chance please?"

Another of pause. Always pauses. Stopping and starting. Stopping and starting.

"Hello? Hello? Yes, I'm still here. Oh, I see. Not Turtle then, but Morricone Crescent? 16—yes, yes. What's that? Dinnridge, you say. Where's that?"

CHAPTER THIRTY-SIX

The orderly at the Domino Wing of Dinnridge Hospital handed Sandy an envelope. "I'm instructed to give you this."

The envelope was A4-sized and brown with 'SANDY AMADEUS' scrawled in large uneven capitals where an address might have been and 'by hand' across the top. Both instructions were double underlined.

"You should read it now," the orderly said.

"You know what it says?"

"My instructions, mister Amadeus are to give it to you, in person, by hand, as it says. To the addressee as it were. That is all."

Sandy opened the envelope, extracted a wad of A4 sheets, stapled together, and sat down next to Angela on a wooden bench in an echoey grey corridor that reeked of stale cigarettes. He read:

Sandy Dear Sandy,
Sandy the innocent, the innocence of the Sandys—
You know, it took me a long time to settle into the journey of my life. Longer than my school mates, for sure. Although to be honest I was always travelling in the right direction, lurching from side to side like

some rattily old railway carriage clanking along not quite straight rails, pushing through hot yellow sun into cold grey rain, up, up, up, and on—up into thunder-black mountains, even switching tracks when opportunities arose. But switching tracks when hauling land from a single point on the horizon makes no difference, in the end. I left the sunshine behind. Damn madam Destiny and Her damn destination!

Pah! You probably want to know how I knew it would be you, reading this *missive*. Sure you do. What da-ya wanna-me ta say? *Because your name is on the envelope!*

I met a philosopher once. He said, "Oh! It's you!" His little joke, now shared.

Kenya. So, Kenya. Ever been to Kenya? Probably not. Not on your CV and why would Vic Victor junior send you? That's where I was born, see. Nyeri County, in the foothills of mount Kenya. That's where it all started.

What do I remember of Kenya? Two things: a wonderful feeling about life, and the event that robbed me of that feeling, forever—and no, I'm not talking child neglect or abuse as shrinks are keen to latch onto these days. No, no, it was, well—give me time to compose myself before touching on what happened.

You think England is a green and pleasant land? I'm sure you do. Green, it is. Temperate, too—who would gainsay *The Two Williams*—Blakey and Shakey?

But that part of Kenya is greener. You think England is green? Now think greener. You think

England is pleasant? Now think pleasanter. Wet a little sometimes, okay, but in Nyeri County wet is warm. It may overwhelm and saturate at times, but it's never a chore.

Green I remember, and warm red soils, and music. I remember songs, *beau-di-lyrical* songs, songs that made choirs of the heart. Picture for me a dozen—no, two dozen—tea-growers and pickers singing around a flaming metal drum. The air is heavy with the smouldering scent of sun-dried sticks and cuttings while, under the starlight of a moon-free sky, this wonderful choir teases joy into the lullaby chuckle of the night.

I was almost eight years old then. Four days after my eighth birthday I was packed off to England to boarding school. I see eight-year-olds today and I think: how could you send one of those, one of your own, thousands of miles away to cold, wet England, to a prison during term time and the custody of a well-meaning but clueless maiden aunt for the holidays?

The answer of course lay in the alternative... but that was long ago. A lifetime ago.

Vic Victor, then, Vic Victor.

You like Vic Victor? A great talent in my opinion. But judge him by what he does, not by my opinion—especially not by other people's opinion, no, no, for all too often the only thing *them mouthy geysers ever done in their whole lives* is give of *the old opinion*. Up there with the Lloyd-Webers of this world, Vic Victor is, I should say. But talent on its own? Never enough.

You do so need good luck. You need madam Destiny on your side. An invisible helping hand. And guts— or chutzpah—those two close comrades at arms, they are your allies. How much art and science has been lost to the world because some bitter, artless bully has amused himself by destroying the vessel that dare kindle the flame of talent? Guts and chutzpah, see, and a dose of good luck, they'll see you through. And better all mankind.

When I saw your graduation gig (*a student wrote that??!!*) I knew you would be the good luck that Vic Victor needed. I had been his good luck once, but good luck ran out on me. My luck took him—us—as far as *Gaius*. Merely the foothills of what might be. He needs the right story and the right lyricist—a star too, if you can rise to that gig—someone with a certain *knack*. That knack, that subtle twisted way with words, something to complement his music, yes, I saw that in you.

It pains me that it took so long to catch up with you after you left Pemberwell. Three years doing lowly jobs off the radar—keep yourself visible, my advice there.

All said and done, though, to this day I owe Vic Victor junior a story. I owe him that, for all the promise I failed to fulfil.

But let me not be mawkish! (Change the subject you burnt out old fart, you.)

Let's talk Rap Banter.

I don't suppose you ever saw Rap Banter. I first saw

them at the Bee Hive. Well, Linda on her own first. Love at first sight.

They didn't have a manager and were playing mid-week. Soul-destroying gig that, if you let it get to you—hardly anyone drinking mid-week (and those that do, want to drink, not listen). I'd already met Vic Victor senior, bumped into Jerry Rubenstein at the same party, and Jerry took *Banter* under his managerial wing. My reward was to hang out with the lovely Linda Turnbull. At some point, though, she took against me. For no reason I ever fathomed. That was before the mugging.

Do you know I witnessed the mugging? Me and Johnny *Guitar* Mersh, on Shepherd's Bush Green in sight of the Empire. I called for the ambulance and kept her warm. He chased the bastard but didn't catch him. Linda's arm was broken. Never played the piano again. Lost any appetite at all for the stage. Of course that doubled my motivation to keep up the super-fan thing. I'd invented Ruby Rattler at that first gig because I was shy. Plain and simple. I wanted Linda to know how great she was.

After the mugging, I suppose I thought, in a child-like way, that she might return to the stage, just to sing. Looking back, you might think it creepy, but really it wasn't. I fed her connections that I knew of from my meanderings through musical theatre land, hoping that somewhere along the line an opportunity would appear that she could grasp.

Anyway, soon we were working together, if less

warmly than I might have hoped, on *Gaius.*

Gaius, as shortly was to become apparent, was the best I'd ever do in my life. We all knew it was the foothills. It could easily be a one-hit-wonder—it might still be that, let's be honest. But it was a thing. We had made a thing, and people were paying money hand-over-fist to share our work with us. This time the whole shemozzle felt right. Everything came together, as if for the first time in our lives we knew what we were doing. Busy, though, busy. Never a moment's peace. We were swinging in the rigging, white-knuckling the ropes night after night for fear of the fall. In the end the fall came, but not in a way that anyone ever imagined.

It was on the back of its early success, even before we'd notched up 250 performances, that I took out the mortgage on the tiny flat in Morricone Crescent. Before we notched up 500, the trouble had started. The trouble was noise.

Okay. I think I have to tell you this now. Linda's mugging gave me flashbacks.

When the scream of a woman shattered the night across Shepherd's Bush Green, and sure as hell as I think of it now, I see a tribesman with a machete running amok slashing wildly, aimlessly, in a frenzy, at the arms and legs and necks of the gorgeous singers in that beautiful plantation choir.

The faces of the grown-ups who were my friends are, in these moments, distorted in terror, splashed with blood, animated, even after death, by the flames from the metal drum. I am thrown into the bushes by

Obuya, the man who saved my life, then I watch him as he is hacked to death while I, praying for invisibility, hide, bewildered at my cowardice.

I was packed off to England for safety, and my parents were right, for worse was to come.

You can weaponise anything, of course. People do.

Today, it is widely known that noise can be used like that. The US played loud rock music to drive Noriega from sanctuary in the Holy See's embassy in Panama.

And thus, to my new flat.

Before Morricone Crescent, I would return home having done my exhausting best in the role of Gaius Julius Caesar and, usually around midnight, I would slip between the sheets, my body limp, my soul weary, but my mind a-buzz with critical analysis, how to maintain the pace of my performance, how to not let the show flag... hoping, as would happen eventually, that all the crazy ideas would talk themselves out and the next thing I'd know it would be 10 a.m. and, fully refreshed, I'd strike out to make the best of the next day.

In Morricone Crescent this did not happen. No sooner had my crazy ideas calmed themselves to a whisper when loud thumping bass would beat its interminable rhythm through my ceiling. Complain? Did I complain? Sure but never was so much complaining about so much noise met with so much rebuttal and justification and eventually indifference but never, ever with effective action.

Any idea of a lie-in to recover from a bad night disappeared with the air-con next door and whatever other equipment had been installed to maintain the sub-basement swimming pool. And that was before the neighbour on the other side started haranguing her interior designers—one of whom, I discovered, committed suicide, naming her at the top of his list of woes.

In the beginning, my performances suffered. Then my attendance. Rumours started to spread about my drinking; I hardly ever touch a drop—I have shows to make which need the body at peak performance. Drinking is out. *Verboten.*

Complain! I hear you say. With these people, to a man, complaint had no effect.

Move! I hear you say. But the flat with such noisy neighbours is worth nothing; I am deep in debt; I have worse than lost everything. Besides, *you would have me dump the problem on someone else's doorstep?* Some said yes, of course. I caught Obuya's dying eye and I did not.

Do something! I said to myself. And I did. I built a sound-proof room inside my front room, to live in.

But too late. I might as well have been a drunk, for not only did I get shunted out of the main role, shunned by my colleagues for bringing the show down, but I now found myself unable to pluck words from the air as one does in normal conversation (Even this *missive*, my dear Sandy, is the umpteenth rewrite, dictionary and thesaurus in hand). My doctor performed a senility check, and was sorry to say...

Yes, the price of sustained sleep deprivation.

So they had killed me.

Just as guerrilla fighters hacked my parents to pieces after I left for England.

My neighbours killed me.

That's what it boiled down to. As I struggled through my day, bleary eyed and *compos-not-so-mentis* I was blessed with the opportunity of passing in the street the exact same people who had condemned me to an early grave and a nasty journey, at that, to that six foot hole of no return.

The theatre, I knew, was on its knees, and all those wonderful hard-working people, rightfully, blamed me for letting them down, because it *was* me who had let them down.

Well, you know what? Sound travels two ways. And if you have a mind to, in that flat, you can hear what people say, not only upstairs but on either side.

Let me be brief: the people upstairs had rented the room above and the lady of the house had taken to banging the lodger and funding his dope habit. Harrietta Dagg, the woman next door, got through on average one interior designer every three weeks, having forced them to fork out for ludicrously extravagant materials and then abandon them to bankruptcy.

My researches were ably assisted by the regular miss-delivery of post, which I started to read instead of politely putting through the correct letter box.

Then there was the hit and run and the 'stolen' car which, following the Ruby Rattler tip-off, I'm sure you got to the truth of. Go through my archives, you're welcome to them. Read all I have, who I wrote to and what I wrote to persuade them to do as they did.

Who would begrudge a dying man vengeance, if not Justice, against those who had slain him? Especially when it was not I that pulled the trigger, but someone similarly aggrieved. I do not seek to exonerate myself, I merely suggest that Justice—when writ large—is by and for the many, not the one.

As I write this, as you read it, I cannot know which of my paybacks has paid off. I think each had a good chance. And if successful, I can probably safely say without sabotaging anything now, that my favourite—as I imagine it played out—would be the vengeance of Crispin Cramptin if he has, as I hoped to seed the thought in his mind, reproduced the stage set he designed for the Cask of Amontillado at the Young Vic, and bricked the Dagg woman up behind a new wall in her own basement with her squawking voice on a loop to listen to as she suffocates. *Ah Poe! You genius!*

(Did the prop man hold a prop gun to Harrietta's head, I wonder?)

That's why all the others wore headphones. Did you spot that? Not only did they have to know they were dying—like me—but their dying deserved its own soundtrack, and not a short one either, but, as near as dammit the noise they, individually, had inflicted on me.

As for Benedetto-in-hiding Luce, I'm guessing he's still alive. You will want to know—heh! the police will want to know, because like any good citizen you must hand this *missive* over to the police, but: *who shall squidge the Benedetto soul out of its unfeeling skin?*

My answer can only, honestly, be vague: All those families touched by the Solino Bridge disaster now know who he is and where he lives, and I ask you: might any one of two hundred or more co-victims of his callous indifference feel disposed to act? That is the question friend Benedetto must ask himself.

How many among us are would-be killers? Murderers *manqué*? One in a hundred? One in a thousand? A million, maybe? What does it take to goad someone to murder? Let me tell you, you will never know unless and until, you yourself are so goaded. High-minded judge-wigged morality is fine. Untested.

So for Benedetto, every time he leaves his front door. Every time he crosses the street. Every time, Benedetto, you sit in the Dolce Vita Café in Jermyn Street and you ostrich your head and sip the americano you are addicted to, will someone whose life you destroyed be there behind you, stiletto in hand?

Sandy, I do not want you to feel used or soiled by any role you may have played in all this. You may feel it, for which I apologise. But beware that feeling. Self-esteem is a treacherous thing. I had to make you a part of these events, somehow, so that whatever story you find for Vic Victor, in the end, it is a story you can authentically claim as your own. Whether this is a gift or a curse is up to you. You have the luxury of that choice because you have a life ahead of you that you can live. I must fulfil my destiny and give Vic Victor junior a story.

Thus I make amends for my failure.

You see, in either action or inaction, I find guilt, and I lack the time to make better, more effective, use of what is left.

Yours, Barry Turtle, aka Ruby Rattler

CHAPTER THIRTY-SEVEN

Sandy, feeling as though someone had just entombed him in concrete, handed the letter to Angela.

"Mister Amadeus, Miss Mistral," the orderly said, "we have a playroom for the child. You may not want her to see..."

Sandy exchanged a look with Angela.

"Okay," Angela said and bent down. "Tangerine darling, we won't be long. See if you can find some nice toys to play with."

Tangerine scowled and wrapped her arms around Angela's leg.

"How bad can it be?" Sandy said.

"You're going to a private room," the orderly said. "Children are not allowed on the main ward. We have visitor's rooms, but in this case, well, as you'll see, visitor's rooms don't apply. You may meet patients on the way, of course."

Equally, Sandy thought, patients might wander into the playroom. He glanced Angela's way with a shrug.

"We'll decide when we get there," she said.

The orderly took them outside and led them across well-kept lawns between accommodation blocks and eventually they came to a detached house, as you might find on any street in any suburb. A nurse let them in and they were escorted to the equivalent of the reception room in a normal house.

The nurse opened the door. She rested her hand on Tangerine's shoulder. "Perhaps not the child?"

"We had to reinforce the floor," the orderly said.

A metre beyond the door, blocking the way, a blue-grey plasterboard wall reached almost to the ceiling and extended left and right between the front and back of the reception room.

Angela squatted to Tangerine's level. "Give us a minute darling."

"If you just squeeze through on the left," the orderly said, "there are French windows at the front."

"What is it?" Sandy said, thinking it was the shape, size and colour of the containment he would expect around the core of a nuclear reactor.

"It's a sound-proof room. Mister Turtle insisted we install it as a condition of his voluntary admission."

"He insisted?" Angela said. "It was up to him?"

"Oh yes. He knew full well what was happening to him. All the more tragic of course. Initially, he wanted to keep noise out. Now, basically, it keeps the sound of his screaming from the other patients."

Sandy shufffled sideways to the front of the room and turned the corner.

There was not one set of French windows at the front of the sound-proof room, but two. They were set back to back, with a 15 cm air gap between them. The sound-proof room itself was a shell within a shell. Sandy reckoned the walls, taken together, must be fifty centimetres thick leaving little room for any-thing, or anyone, inside. The inside was pipe-room small, in fact.

A man sat at a fold-down table. He was facing the wall with his head in his hands. A single bulb at the centre of the ceiling cast his shadow across the table top where it blurred into his elbows.

"He's shaking," Sandy said.

"That's the medication," the orderly said. "Calms him down."

"Can I talk to him?"

"He won't hear you," the orderly said. "He cut off his ears and has excised his own eardrums, beyond repair. Did that weeks ago. We have to give him painkillers for the pain—they keep getting infected because he scratches them so much. But we can't give him anything for the tinnitus. It's the tinnitus that makes him scream. Plagues him night and day. Sleeps terribly badly, and that makes the dementia worse. As best we know he was tortured. God forgive me, but if I knew who did this to this poor creature, I'd be struck off for what I'd do to them."

"Can I go in?" Sandy said.

The orderly flicked a switch to flash the light.

The man looked up at the three of them in the window.

For a fraction of a second it was as if he recognised them. But it was only fleeting because now his mouth opened, the flesh of his nose crinkled, his eyes nar-rowed, and the black dots at their centres widened in unfocused rage. His face became that of a demon from Bosch or Breughel—the face of a demon suffering the red hot pain of a poker plunged deep into the crevace between his buttocks—and you could hear the scream, the distant scream, the scream of the kid next door, as he rolls on the pavement, three blocks away, being knifed.

The creature ran at the glass of the door. He ran with his head down. He ran as if hitting the glass hard enough would stop the pain.

The top of the head met the glass. There was an audible thud. The glass flexed and the French window shunted forward ten centimetres or more out of line with the wall.

He fell in a crumpled heap on the thick carpet.

The orderly thumped a red mushroom-button.

An alarm bell rattled into life.

The nurse pushed Sandy out of the way.

He watched in horror as a shock-absorbing mechanism returned the inner window to its proper position, ready for next time. The nurse was already through the door and checking Barry Turtle's pulse, fixing a collar to his neck, stroking his matted hair.

"Sorry. Thought he was over doing that. Been a few of weeks since he played bull to the glass matador. He'll have to go back to wearing the scrum cap," the orderly said. "He won't like that. Don't think you want to go in, do you?"

*   *   *

On their way out they met Linda Turnbull.

She was ashen faced.

"It's him, isn't it?" She said.

Sandy nodded.

"It was him all the time," she said. She sat down on the hard wooden bench. "I don't think I can bear to look him in the eye."

CHAPTER THIRTY-EIGHT

"You have to identify Rupert's body," Sandy said, walking back from the woman police officer at the Perspex window.

They were in the public reception area at the police station in Ladbroke Grove, giving themselves up, as it were.

"Surely he has a relative," Angela said. "He'll surely have hundreds when they find out about the house in Notting Hill."

"They seem to think you're married to him."

"I most certainly am not!"

"From what I can tell," Sandy said, "which you are about to find out, all official like, they think you are Tangerine's mother, too."

"No daughter of mine could be as white as her!"

"You'd best take it up with them. But, before you make too much fuss, and God knows what Rupert was up to, but maybe, just maybe, you might want to accept the discovery gracefully?"

"Oh yes? And how do I explain that I didn't come clean before?"

"Fear," Sandy said. "Pure fear. You had to pretend, in case you were next. You didn't know which way to turn. Who or what was safe and how safe, or whatever."

"No. We'd never pull it off."

"We don't have to. It's already been done."

Angela ran her fingers through her hair. Bunched it and released it.

"Morally," Sandy said, "don't you own that house anyway?"

"And Tangerine?"

"A mother knows best."

He watched Angela closely. He had his story, some version of the events that Barry had orchestrated. And with a story in his hand that only he could tell he had every chance of getting to write at least some of the songs. What more could he want?

He watched Angela and Tangerine playing a finger game. Angela's fingers were slim and delicate. Her skin the golden brown of... a simple wonder captivated his senses. The right words would not be his today.

Angela didn't like it.

Rupert Ulan Mikov Malinbrough had played her all the way. She had been a puppet, worse still, he had designs on her as a sexual toy. And now, even though, just possibly, the house in some moral sense belonged to her; she had not earned it, and in truth, in fact, she did not own it. She had not properly inherited it. She had not honestly received it even as a gift.

If she accepted the house—and the marriage—she would live the rest of her life a lie. Always on the verge of being found out. And knowing it herself.

Besides, she didn't want a house. She didn't want

possessions as such, she wanted to be the person she might be, to be a creative participant in the real world. Hiding away in some ivory tower, preciously guarding a safe-load of gold, that was not her. That was not what life was about. So, no: she would not accept the house. She would disarm it as a fact, a temptation, a weapon to torture her conscience, make it neutral. Somehow.

As for Tangerine, if there was anything in the world she was sure of, you can't play possessions with people's souls. Especially not children. What she needed to do was place her relationship with Tangerine on a proper-for-Angela legal footing. That of course would be difficult because the authorities here like the authorities everywhere insist on procedural-ising everything. As soon as you proceduralise some-thing, you de-humanise it.

And so going to the authorities for Tangerine would be self-defeating. No, she would take legal advice, play a slow game, bit by bit day by day she would change the situation until she was with all authenticity Tan-gerine's mother, and the mistress of her own life. A designer designing.

She turned to Sandy who had just taken Tangerine onto his knee. "For one who craves the authentic," she said, "you give in to temptation very quickly. So no. We will find a better way. This is about my story, not yours."

The female officer returned to the counter. "Angela Malin... Bruff? I have the address for you. To identify the deceased."

*   *   *

Moe Stone had the front page spread in the first edition of *The Inspector*, the latest addition to the British Sunday Papers.

The headline 'Poe-Faced Dagg Digs Own Grave' dwarfed even the self-serving 'Taylor Takes on Telegraph and Times' about the launch of Stamford Taylor's new newspaper. Moe's piece included an exclusive photograph of Dagg leaving Pimlico police station, having been cautioned over the discovery of a second walled-up room and a second corpse, behind the recently exposed murder room in which his daughter died.

The last piece in the puzzle, as with so many things in life, had been the first piece he had found, which Dagg had uncovered when he went through his old, unpublished filings, looking for references to Matterhorn.

A copy of an old planning application for 14 Morricone Crescent had turned up. Plans submitted by Harrietta made the basement out to be smaller than the first floor by half a metre. Enough to hide a body. He suggested the police excavate beyond Crispin Cramptin's brickwork. They had.

Today, Moe was a hero for holding out for the truth, for standing up to Dagg, for taking the bull out of bullying—as he liked to think.

That first weekend the paper sold out its print run, while the competition filled its pages with self-flagellation and the vilification of the royal family over the death of Diana: *The Inspector sold out!*

He was not sure, however, that he was ready to give up canal life. It had kind of grown on him, and perhaps he could take things more slowly now. Now he could pick and choose his cases... and there were others from his past that might be worth chasing up; many more old chickens that were coming home to roost; there was Crime City London that his new mate Stamford was taking an interest in.

He had only to dig around a bit.

It took several days and, by Friday, Linda had summoned the courage to see Barry *Ruby Rattler* Turtle who, she supposed, was her man in prison.

Whether Sandy would be the saviour of the theatre company had yet to be seen. But why not? During the course of that week, he turned in his first treatment of a story, and Vic Victor had read it start to finish without putting it down. What the story was, Linda had yet to find out.

Sandy's story could wait till Monday.

First thing Saturday morning she went back to Dinnridge, to see Barry.

She went through the main entrance at 9 a.m. on the dot. Determined that she would face the man who changed her life, and thank him. And beg forgiveness.

She met the orderly she'd seen previously.

But Barry had gone.

Also published by The Logic of Dreams

An anthology of all new crime and mystery stories, edited by Jack Calverley.

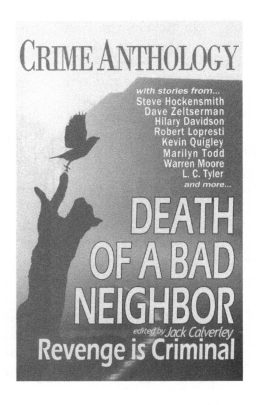

CRIME ANTHOLOGY

with stories from...
Steve Hockensmith
Dave Zeltserman
Hilary Davidson
Robert Lopresti
Kevin Quigley
Marilyn Todd
Warren Moore
L. C. Tyler
and more...

DEATH
OF A BAD
NEIGHBOR
edited by Jack Calverley
Revenge is Criminal

Available from the usual bookstores or through:
doabn.com

Also published by The Logic of Dreams

CB's Top 100 Writing Tips, Tricks, Techniques and Tools from the Advice Toolbox / Writing Fiction Bottom Up [Amazon edition]

Available from the usual bookstores or through:
carterblakelaw.com